I0541109

The
Space
Between

Stephanie Casher

The Pantheon Collective (TPC)
www.pantheoncollective.com

The Pantheon Collective (TPC)
P.O. Box 799
Santa Cruz, CA 95061

The Space Between. Copyright © 2015 by Stephanie Casher
All rights reserved.

PUBLISHER'S NOTE
This book is a work of fiction. Names, characters, places and
incidents either are the product of the author's imagination or
are used fictitiously, and any resemblance to actual persons, living
or dead, business establishments, events, or locales is entirely
coincidental.

Without limiting the rights under copyright reserved above, no part
of this publication may be reproduced, stored in, or introduced
into a retrieval system, or transmitted, in any form, or by any means
(electronic, mechanical, photocopying, recording, or otherwise),
without the prior written permission of both the copyright owner
and the above publisher of this book.

The scanning, uploading, and distribution of this book via the
Internet or via any other means without the permission of the
publisher is illegal and punishable by law. Please purchase only
authorized electronic editions, and do not participate in or encourage
electronic piracy of copyrighted materials. Your support of the
author's rights is appreciated.

ISBN: 978-0-9965318-0-1 (Paperback)
ISBN: 978-0-9965318-1-8 (Ebook)

Printed in United States of America

Cover: Designed by Marion Designs
Interior: Designed by Stephanie Casher

The
Space
Between

Stephanie Casher

The Pantheon Collective (TPC)
www.pantheoncollective.com

The Pantheon Collective (TPC)
P.O. Box 799
Santa Cruz, CA 95061

The Space Between. Copyright © 2015 by Stephanie Casher
All rights reserved.

PUBLISHER'S NOTE
This book is a work of fiction. Names, characters, places and
incidents either are the product of the author's imagination or
are used fictitiously, and any resemblance to actual persons, living
or dead, business establishments, events, or locales is entirely
coincidental.

Without limiting the rights under copyright reserved above, no part
of this publication may be reproduced, stored in, or introduced
into a retrieval system, or transmitted, in any form, or by any means
(electronic, mechanical, photocopying, recording, or otherwise),
without the prior written permission of both the copyright owner
and the above publisher of this book.

The scanning, uploading, and distribution of this book via the
Internet or via any other means without the permission of the
publisher is illegal and punishable by law. Please purchase only
authorized electronic editions, and do not participate in or encourage
electronic piracy of copyrighted materials. Your support of the
author's rights is appreciated.

ISBN: 978-0-9965318-0-1 (Paperback)
ISBN: 978-0-9965318-1-8 (Ebook)

Printed in United States of America

Cover: Designed by Marion Designs
Interior: Designed by Stephanie Casher

For Phyllis (aka Mom), Aunt Mae, and Aaronette

This world just isn't the same without you...

The *Soul Mates* Series

Acknowledgements

This book is dedicated to the fans of *When Love Isn't Enough*. To every single person who has wrote or facebooked me, inquiring about when the sequel was coming out... every person who has been waiting patiently, for years, to see what happens next. You guys were my motivation throughout this entire process, as I struggled through some difficult personal times to get this book done. For you. So that you could lay hands on a story that you felt was worth the wait. I am so grateful for your patience, and for still being here, wanting to read my stuff! As an author, there are few things that feel better than someone pulling you aside to tell you how much they loved your book. If you ever took the time out to do that for me, whether through a message or review, please know you provided me with a priceless moment. The ultimate validation for a creative soul. I cannot begin to express how much your support means to me.

And to my husband, my partner in all things: I couldn't do any of this without you. Well, technically, I could... but it wouldn't be nearly as much fun. ;) xoxo

*F*rom the terrace of my hotel suite, I stared down at the collection of people gathered to witness our nuptials. It was a small ceremony, nothing fancy, with only our nearest and dearest in attendance. In a few minutes, it would be time to head down to the beach, in my strapless white gown, to become Mrs. Damion Waters.

Panic gripped my rapidly beating heart. *I don't think I can go through with this.*

Not because I didn't love him—I loved Damion with all my heart. He was my *best* friend, a truly amazing man. I'd never had someone so devoted to my care and comfort. But that spark, that out of control, life-consuming fire—it just wasn't there. I'd tried to convince myself that a steady, solid, reliable love was more important than passion, but after much soul-searching, I had come face to face with the fact that I was kidding myself. Settling. Maybe if I'd never known that kind of passion, I wouldn't miss it so much. But I knew what it felt like to love someone so much you could barely breathe, and no matter how hard I tried, I couldn't forget.

Damn you, Tony. Damn you, damn you, damn you.

My sister, Megan, came up behind me, resting her hand on the small of my back. "You about ready?" she asked.

I set my bouquet of calla lilies on the table. "Can you get Damion for me?"

"Isn't it bad luck for the groom to see the bride before the wedding?"

"Meg, I don't think there's going to be a wedding…"

1

Chapter One

Samantha

Three years earlier…

I've tried really hard to live my life with honor and integrity, especially when it comes to matters of the heart. After all, the heart is a fragile thing, the seat of human vulnerability, our Achilles heel. A major break can do irreparable damage, and I'm speaking from experience on this one, having lived through the after effects of an all-consuming, life-wrecking love affair.

When I was 19-years-old, I met the man who I believed to be my soulmate. We had that magical chemistry you see in movies; the moment we laid eyes on each other for the first time, we just *knew*. Up to that point, I was somewhat of a cynic—my first "love" had ended in heartbreak and completely damaged my ability to trust. But the connection I shared with Tony, said soulmate, was not something I could deny. And believe me, I tried. There are just some people who, once they get hooks into your heart, are impossible to shake.

Yes, it's always exciting to meet the man of your dreams, and discovering he returns your feelings is all kinds of euphoric. Fate

3

at work. But the path to our happy ending wasn't exactly clear. Tony came with a rather significant complication—a girlfriend. A girlfriend who, for reasons I still struggle to understand, he found it difficult to sever ties with. Tony, bless his non-confrontational, peace-loving heart, couldn't stand the thought of hurting anyone. As Damion used to say, this was Tony's best and worst quality.

Damion—a tall, dark, dreadlocked Adonis—was Tony's best friend. When we met, Damion was in his fourth year as a graduate student in the History of Consciousness Ph.D. program at UC Santa Cruz, where we all went to school. Damion is one of those impossibly smart, activist-oriented, hip-hop intellectuals; his insightful critiques of the establishment were reminiscent of KRS-One and Public Enemy. Heavily influenced by the psychologist Frantz Fanon, he double-majored in History and Psychology at the University of Oregon and was now writing his dissertation on the psychology of the oppressed and the absence of contemporary social movements in the United States.

Damion's greatest passion was the empowerment of underrepresented minorities in underserved communities, and he was committed to using his voice to speak out against all forms of injustice. An accomplished orator and professional keynote/ emcee, he could frequently be found onstage at some event, mic in hand, trying to incite the next revolution. He never passed up an opportunity to drop knowledge and wisdom on impressionable, young minds. Possessing hypnotic charisma, Damion would open his mouth and audiences would fall in rapture. To this day, I've never met someone with greater powers of persuasion.

Damion also gave awesome hugs, which I took advantage of on many occasions while I waited for Tony to figure things out. When Tony finally managed to free himself from his relationship with Angela, we embarked on what was supposed to be a long and passionate journey together. But Angela had other plans. A series of tragic events drove a wedge between Tony and me, turning us into star-crossed lovers. Convinced that we were destined to be together, I put my life on hold and waited for him… refusing to give up on the future we had planned.

During our estrangement, Tony and I did most of our communicating through Damion, and Damion provided a strong, supportive shoulder for me to cry on during those long, hard months. Honestly, I don't know if I would have made it through that phase of my life without Damion. During the lowest of the lows, he was a true friend, and over time, I came to rely on him.

Tony never made it back to me, and I was left devastated and heartbroken. I truly believed he was *The One*; it never occurred to me that there were forces in this world strong enough to keep soulmates apart. That maybe true love *couldn't* conquer all. I don't know what was more tragic—losing Tony, or losing the part of me that still believed in true love and the possibility of happily ever after.

In the wake of Tony's abandonment, Damion and I built upon our budding friendship. My wounds were still pretty raw, deep lacerations that refused to scab over. To guard against infection, I decided to keep people, men especially, at a distance. I was determined to protect myself by any means necessary. But for some reason, my defense mechanisms never kicked in when

Damion was around. I've always felt completely safe with him, and his tender, loving care played a huge part in my healing.

Damion was also a fantastic influence on me scholastically. While I worked toward my BA in Sociology, Damion was finishing up his dissertation and trying to line up a job in preparation for his inevitable entry into the real world. He was so focused and driven, quite the contrast to my peers who were more interested in partying than planning for the future. I found myself emulating his work ethic and attitude towards academics, and earned straight-A's my junior and senior years.

We never spoke about Tony. Of course I was curious, but I knew better than to open that door again. Tony had made his choice (if you could even call it a choice), and I had vowed not to waste another moment with my life on hold. There had been enough of that nonsense.

Somewhere along the way, Damion developed a crush on me, which we came very close to acting on while I was rebounding from Tony. But deep down, I knew it was wrong. Not only were Tony and Damion like brothers, but I was in no position to return Damion's feelings. Damion had been such a good friend to me; it wasn't right to use him as a distraction. Which is all he could have been because I was still very much in love with his best friend.

Damion was the perfect gentleman and never pressed the issue, appearing content with the platonic bond we'd forged. I'd see him once or twice a week and we'd go hiking, to the movies, or catch a show downtown at the Catalyst. I actually credit him with bringing the fun back into my world after a long bout of depression and hibernation.

"Come on," he said, dragging me towards the Rock-O-Plane, one of his favorite rides at the Santa Cruz Beach Boardwalk. "We have time for one more ride before the show starts."

Steel cages dangled from the limbs of the Ferris wheel towering above us. "I don't know, Dame. That might be a little too much spinning for my current state of intoxication."

"Oh, you'll be fine," he said.

He was always saying that, "you'll be fine." Right before he nudged (or shoved) me outside of my comfort zone.

"Alright, but if I puke all over your Jordan's, it's on you. Literally."

I managed to keep the contents of my stomach where they belonged, and after a laughter-filled spin on the Rock-O-Plane, we headed down to the beach for the show. Every Friday night the Boardwalk hosted a free concert on the beach, and the line-up was great for the nostalgia factor. So far we'd seen Eddie Money, the Family Stone (minus Sly), and the Gin Blossoms. Tonight's entertainment would be provided by 90's pop queen, Tiffany.

We had a blast drinking beer and singing along to her cheesy (but classic) tunes like "I Think We're Alone Now." I hadn't heard that song in years, yet still knew *every word*. To my amusement, I discovered Damion knew every word as well. That was one of the lovely paradoxes about Damion—while he was smart, studious, and articulate enough to hold his own in a debate with Cornel West, he was still able to access his inner 10-year-old with ease. The man could put in work, but also knew how to play, as accomplished in the art of silliness as any other subject.

As my Junior year drew to a close, Damion successfully defended his dissertation and was preparing to head to London. He'd been offered a postdoctoral fellowship at Goldsmiths University, where he planned to conduct research for a comparative study on U.S. and UK youth uprisings. This was an amazing opportunity for him, and I shared his excitement. But as his departure date drew near, the magnitude of what this meant for our friendship began to sink in. Damion, my faithful companion and BFF, was moving to *London*.

A week before his departure, we took one final trek into the Pogonip, a heavily forested state park adjacent to the UCSC campus. Our ritual was to hike deep into the woods and pause for a smoke break underneath our favorite tree, Papa Wood. In the book, *The Celestine Prophecy*, James Redfield claimed that old-growth redwoods were a critical source of energy that people could tap into to increase their own personal reserves. Papa Wood, whose trunk was easily twelve feet in diameter, definitely fell into the "old-growth" category and we'd spent many afternoons with our backs against his sturdy trunk, meditating on the mysteries of life.

Damion took a seat and passed me his palm-sized glass pipe, the bowl packed with Santa Cruz's finest tasty greens. I took a hit and passed the pipe back to him, a stream of smoke passing over my lips as I exhaled.

"I can't believe this is our last session under this tree," Damion said.

"Don't remind me." I was enjoying my bubble of denial about Damion's departure, not yet ready for the inevitable burst.

"I don't think they have redwood forests in England," he

mused. "I wonder what I'll do when I need to replenish my energy. I've been spoiled living in Santa Cruz so long. Folks are of a very high spiritual caliber here."

"If there are spiritual folks to be found, I have no doubt you will draw them to you. You're a magnet when it comes to that stuff." And it was the truth. Damion was a living, breathing poster child for the Law of Attraction—he put peaceful, positive vibes out into the Universe on a regular basis and was continuously blessed with opportunity and good fortune. I truly believed my life had been improved by sheer proximity, and was worried that his departure would trigger a depressive doom spiral.

"Won't be the same without my wing woman," he said with a wink.

"Maybe now you'll be able to find yourself a lady friend who can offer more perks than companionship," I teased.

Damion's smile faded, his brows bending toward the center of his face. "Still won't be the same."

I'd tried many times to encourage Damion to take a dip in the dating pool, but he always had an excuse handy:

"These days, dating and drama go hand in hand. Who's got time for that?"

"A girlfriend will just distract me from the work I need to do on my dissertation."

"It doesn't make sense to start a relationship right now—I'm getting ready to leave the country."

And so on. While those were all valid points, I always suspected there was more to it, like he was still carrying a torch for me. Which is why I frequently tried to direct his affection elsewhere.

9

But now that his attention was about to be permanently reassigned as he was physically removed from my sphere, separation anxiety was setting in. The more I contemplated "Life without Damion," the more I realized how attached I'd become over the past year. Without any drama or complications, we'd been fulfilling each other's need for companionship and emotional connection. His absence was going to create a huge void in my life, and I was starting to freak out. Isn't that the way it always is though? You never realize how much something means to you until you're on the verge of losing it...

Chapter Two

Samantha

Damion's last night in Santa Cruz was very emotional. I dread goodbyes—they always bring me back to the day Tony left. But this one was particularly hard because the person I usually turned to for comfort and support was the one leaving.

Damion was a beloved member of the UCSC community, and his going-away party was festive and well-attended by students and faculty alike. His mother even flew in from Los Angeles, and it was wonderful to see her again. I had met Damion's mother for the first time when Damion had taken me down to LA for my final showdown with Tony. It was during this trip that I realized a future with Tony was no longer a possibility, and Mama Waters (as she is affectionately known) was a great comfort to me, even though Tony is like a son to her.

As I sat on the porch that July night, almost a year ago, Mama Waters sat down beside me with a pot of chamomile tea. I clutched the warm mug between my palms, holding on for dear life. My tears hadn't stopped flowing since Tony drove away; I was inconsolable.

Damion had been a wonderful support, driving me down to LA for the confrontation, against his better judgment, but I'll never forget how comforting it was to have the company and counsel of another woman at that moment of intense fragility. You see, Tony hadn't just left me, he had left me with child... I didn't share the details of my plight with her, but for some reason I sensed that Mama Waters understood the depth of my agony, the severity of my wound. She didn't press, preach, or judge. In fact, she barely spoke at all, except to impart these timeless words of wisdom:

"Things don't always turn out like we planned, and that's okay. You have to trust that there's a bigger plan at work. We are always being prepared for something better, or protected from something worse." She patted my hand. "We may not see it at the time, but I promise you, it's true."

Those words served as my mantra during my darkest days.

Her outlook on life was remarkable considering all she'd been through. Mama Waters was the epitome of grace under pressure. A single mother, she had raised Damion and his brother in one of the roughest neighborhoods in South Central Los Angeles, where the life expectancy of black males was painfully short. She experienced this firsthand when her firstborn son, Khalil, was gunned down in a gang-related shooting a few months before his 16th birthday. Determined to save Damion from a similar fate, she worked two jobs to earn enough money to move them to a safer neighborhood in a better school district. Damion was all she had left and she would not let him become a statistic.

Mama Waters hadn't walked the easiest of roads, but the years of struggle made moments like this all the more poignant. Damion, her baby boy, had beat the odds. He was now the recipient of a Ph.D., *Doctor* Damion Waters. Not bad for a boy from the hood. But what was truly impressive is that he was just getting started. Damion's idealism and activist bent were the real deal—he was determined to make a difference in this world. He wasn't content to settle on a career, he wanted to build a *legacy*.

Every guest at Damion's going away party that offered a toast (and there were many) spoke of how Damion had changed their life. Helped them see something in a different light. Damion, having inherited his mother's positive outlook, had a calming effect on people. The ability to bring peace to others with his mere presence was Damion's special gift, one that was much appreciated since there was no shortage of people out there doing thoughtless, fucked up shit to each other. But not Damion. He made everything better, and asked for very little in return. Which only made him more beloved.

Mama Waters stood proudly in the corner as love and appreciation was showered upon her son. The speeches went on and on until Damion refocused the love in his mother's direction, giving credit where credit was due. We were all holding back tears as he expressed his love and admiration for his mother, clearly the driving force behind every ounce of greatness he aspired to.

"This woman," Damion proclaimed as his mom tried to shake the blush from her cheeks. "She sacrificed so much, every step of the way, so that I could have access to opportunities for a better life. The greatest gift you can give your kids is the chance to chase their dreams. I'm a project kid; I'm not supposed to be here, with fancy letters after my name, poised to wield actual power against the establishment. And I wouldn't be here without the love, support, and guidance of this incredible woman, my mother, Mrs. Corrine Waters.

"Ma, thank you for all you sacrificed to get me here. For putting a roof over my head and putting me through school. For always putting me first. For teaching me that there is nobility in selflessness. I do this all for, and because of, you."

The room erupted in applause. Raising a man of that caliber is no small feat, and we all owed Mrs. Waters a tremendous debt of gratitude.

Damion stopped by my house before he hit the road, his last stop before bidding farewell to the Cruz. I admit, I was tempted not to answer the door, hoping Damion would refuse to leave town if I denied him the opportunity to say a proper goodbye. I'd never experienced such severe separation anxiety, not even with Tony. It could be years before we saw each other again, and the reality of what that meant was finally starting to hit me.

I know, codependent, much?

"London's just so *far*, you know?" I pouted.

"It is," he said. "But think of it this way—now you have somewhere to stay if you ever decide to visit Europe."

"I may just take you up on that. A flight to London sounds like a great graduation present." I forced a smile. Having something to look forward to, no matter how impractical, made parting a bit easier.

As he pulled me into an embrace, I tried not to think about how this was our *last* hug. But my emotions eventually got the best of me as tears escaped my eyes and hurried down my cheeks to soak the sleeve of his shirt.

"I'm going to miss you so much," I whispered. "You're one of the best friends I've ever had."

Damion stepped back and wiped the tears away with his thumb. "No matter where I am in this world, I will *always* have your back. But you're going to be fine." He planted a kiss on my cheek. "You're a lot stronger than you think."

I wasn't feeling particularly strong at the moment, but I *wanted* to be the brave woman Damion saw when he looked at me. Was I really ready to stand on my own two feet, with no crutches or shoulders to lean on?

I was about to find out.

Chapter Three

Damion

Samantha will never know how close I came to *not* boarding that flight to London.

When I felt the first trace of moisture on her cheek, I was done. What was I doing? Was I really trying to be an ocean away from the woman I loved? It didn't make any damn sense.

Not that she knew I loved her. No, that just would have made things awkward as she mourned the loss of the love of her life, my best friend, Tony Carteris.

Fucking Tony. He had really messed this one up—for all of us. If he had done right by Samantha the first time around, I never would have been put in this position. Tony saw her first, and loved her first, and would have had my full support in riding off into the proverbial sunset with this amazing girl. But for some reason, he had the hardest time manning up and handling his business, i.e., Angela.

Ugh, *that* girl. The anti-Samantha. Selfish, conniving, a professional victim. Angela had Tony twisted up in knots of guilt and obligation

16

and it just wasn't right. The two of them were trapped in a toxic, dysfunctional relationship, the most miserable existence. I'll never understand why Tony chose to forgo light and true love for something dark and seeped in despair.

After Tony broke up with Samantha (in the coldest, cruelest way possible), he asked me to look after her. Make sure she was all right. In Tony's defense, he did truly believe that pushing Samantha away so she could move on and find happiness was in her best interests. But deep down, he knew he'd done a fucked up thing and caused Samantha unnecessary pain. I guess Tony figured anointing her personal protector would ease some of his guilt. How was he, or I, supposed to know I'd end up falling for her, too?

Samantha is an easy person to love. Smart and beautiful, compassionate and kind, she possessed the emotional fortitude of someone twice her age. My attraction to her was instantaneous, and while I tried and tried to fight it, the feelings only grew as time wore on.

As you can imagine, Tony was *not* happy when he learned about my little crush. Yes, I violated guy code by falling for my best friend's girl, but it's not like I acted on it. Even if I wanted to, there was no room for me in Samantha's heart—she was in love with my best friend.

She's *still* in love with my best friend.

I'm not big on unrequited love, so fleeing to Europe seemed like a great way to keep the situation from escalating. I had received fellowship offers from both Cornell University and UCLA, but Goldsmiths in London was the one that served dual purposes. Not

17

only would I be able to conduct ethnographic research in a country with a long history of civil unrest, but 5500 miles was exactly the kind of distance I needed to get control of my feelings and try, as futile as those attempts may be, to get over Samantha.

I hoped the time and space would heal my relationship with Tony as well. Tony had been my best friend since I was 12-years-old. After my brother was killed, my mother took on a second job and moved us to an apartment complex in Santa Monica. Tony lived next door to us with his mother and younger sister, Ashley. Since my mom and Tony's mom were both single, women of color in a predominantly-white neighborhood, they fused a bond that was even stronger than friendship—they formed a sisterhood. And Tony and I, raised side by side, became brothers.

Losing my older brother was one of the most traumatic experiences of my life, and Tony played a big part in helping me rebound from the trauma. With him and Ashley to run around with, I never felt like an only child. Tony could never take my brother's place, but we were tight. We remained inseparable through Middle School and High School, until I left LA to attend the University of Oregon.

Tony's mother passed while I was away at school, and I always felt terrible that I wasn't there for him when he was grieving, the way he'd been there for me. But Angela stepped up in my absence, and when I returned to LA three years later, they were involved in a pretty serious relationship. I remember being surprised when Tony told me he and Angela were dating. We'd all grown up together in a tight neighborhood clique, and I'd always considered Angela one of the guys. Not that she wasn't attractive, but once a girl becomes a "homie," she ceases to be an object of desire. But after graduation, the majority of us went away to college and something changed. Tony and Angela, who elected to stay local and attend Santa Monica City College, formed a legit twosome and deepened their bond.

Going away to college had broadened my horizons, and staying in LA seemed to have the opposite effect on Tony. He was stagnant and appeared to be settling in many areas of his life. I don't necessarily believe that Angela was the *cause* of this stagnation, but let's be real, spending your early twenties in a serious relationship can totally counteract growth. If your partner is not on a similar trajectory, and you're pledging to do everything together, where does that leave you?

For example, Angela was not exactly what I'd call a dreamer. Her mother was a crack addict who would disappear for long stretches of time, leaving her teenage daughter to fend for herself. Since Angela's childhood had been filled with turmoil and upheaval, she yearned for constancy the way some people yearn for freedom. Don't get me wrong—I totally understand why she feels that way. But Angela's fear of change has always been a weight around Tony's ankle, holding him back.

When I returned to California to start the Ph.D. program at UC Santa Cruz, I encouraged Tony to apply to UCSC and finally get that degree he'd been postponing. My hope was that a change of scenery would provide him with renewed inspiration. We had a few good years running around Santa Cruz together (what we jokingly referred to as an 'Angela-free zone'), before Samantha entered the picture and changed everything.

STEPHANIE CASHER

I still can't believe it's been over a year since Tony and I have spoken. Because of a woman. We should be ashamed of ourselves. But despite the way we left things, Tony would eventually get over the urge to knock me out, and I'd have my brother back. I just needed to give him a little more time.

Chapter Four

Damion

When I arrived in London, I experienced culture shock on multiple levels. Not only was I in a foreign country on another continent, but I was living in an urban area again after many years in the idyllic small town of Santa Cruz. The towering redwoods had been replaced with tall buildings, the sidewalks filled with people rushing to and fro. The language was another thing I had to get used to. Even though folks were speaking English, there were many British expressions I needed translated the first time I heard them.

The accents on those British chicks were sexy as hell though.

One pleasant surprise, however, was the diversity I found in London. The city had a substantial immigrant population, and Black and brown faces were in abundance thanks to migration patterns from Africa and the West Indies. It was quite the contrast to the predominantly vanilla landscape in Santa Cruz, and one I appreciated.

Goldsmiths was located in a district in southeast London called New Cross. The school had a Liberal Arts emphasis, and the student body was made up of artists, activists, and the creatively inclined. In this way, the vibe was very similar to Santa Cruz, but more diverse due to the international composition of the student body and faculty. After a few days wandering around in observer mode, I realized I had absolutely made the right choice in coming here.

To ease my transition, I opted for on-campus housing to serve as home base while I got my bearings. I shared a two-room flat with this cat named Jimmy who was getting his Ph.D. in Political Science. Jimmy's family had immigrated to Great Britain from Senegal in the 1970s, and I was sure that our shared levels of melanin would foster an instant bond. However, our first meeting didn't go exactly as I'd hoped.

"American, eh?" he asked, after I introduced myself.

"Yes, from California."

First there was the nod. And then the look. A mixture of pity, distrust, and a tinge of disgust. I would get this look a lot as I traveled throughout Europe. Thanks to Bush, anti-American sentiment abroad was at an all-time high. Quite a change from the WWII days when the United States led the charge and emerged victorious in a global battle against *evil*. But it's a very different story now. The rest of the world was growing tired of the United States' proliferating delusions of grandeur, and folks were not afraid to tell me as much. I actually agreed with most of their criticism, so my citizenship wasn't held against me for too long, but it was strange to have to dispel the "Ugly American" stigma on a daily basis. As a black male, I'd grown up in one of the most marginalized groups in my country; I was used to battling stereotypes and erroneous presumptions everywhere I went. I never imagined it was possible to feel even *more* marginalized than I did as a black man in America.

Jimmy gave me a hard time at first, but I eventually won him over. After I convinced him that I wasn't a selfish, spoiled American with entitlement issues, we got to know each other. It was actually a fortuitous pairing because Jimmy was an expert on the political systems throughout Europe. He was also an immigrant, so he had a unique perspective on race relations in the UK. He provided me with a comprehensive overview of the different castes in English culture, how the various ethnic communities were mapped geographically, and how folks really felt about living under the rule of a monarch. He was more informative than any travel guide or history book, and our conversations were truly eye-opening.

Jimmy was also a DJ, and quite the fixture in London's underground hip hop scene. He had a gig every weekend, and as his roommate, I enjoyed VIP treatment up in the club—another awesome perk. One night we'd be partying at the Amersham Arms in New Cross, another we'd be across town in the West End. London's nightlife was hopping, and I was all up in the mix.

The club was actually a great place to meet folks. Most of the people I'd met on campus were academics-in-training, so my club excursions provided the best opportunities to mingle with the masses. The diversity in London never ceased to amaze me. From what I'd seen on the BBC, I thought England was populated with old, proper white people. Boy was I wrong. London is a transient hub, and there were people here from all walks of life—locals, students, tourists from all over the world—every one of them with a story to tell or a dream they were chasing. I was fascinated and eager to soak up every bit of this strange, new land.

I admit, in those initial weeks, I probably spent *too* much time in the club. Guess I was making up for lost time. Surrounding myself with people and getting lost in the throngs of sweaty, gyrating bodies also helped to combat the loneliness and sporadic homesickness that would creep in during the wee hours of the night. And the women... Good lord. Now there were some beautiful women in Santa Cruz, but most of them were just a variation on the earthy, bohemian goddess. Thankfully I find that type pretty attractive, so I never had any complaints, but what I was exposed to my first few nights in London damn near blew my mind. All the women I came across were so *exotic*, hailing from regions of the world I'd only dreamed of visiting. In my first week, I took every opportunity to strike up conversation with these sultry ambassadors:

Carina – a model from Brazil.

Eleanor – a feisty, blond journalist from Australia in town on assignment.

Hannah and Helga – Twins from Sweden (have mercy!) in town on holiday.

Joy – a foreign exchange student from the Dominican Republic studying at Oxford for the year.

Kimiko – An ExPat from Japan who was working at the Japanese Embassy.

And sexy ass accents on every damn one of them.

Needless to say, I was enjoying the international buffet of loveliness. In addition to being one of those "once in a lifetime" adventures, it kept me from fixating on Samantha. Because at the end of the day, I'd been struck by the same affliction Tony had—I was sprung. Except my situation was worse, I was sprung on a woman who would never love me.

I had a blast exploring my new home. The public transportation system in London is top notch, and I could hop on the "Tube" in New Cross and be in the heart of London in fifteen minutes. I thought it would be difficult living in a new city without my own vehicle, but between the whole "driving on the wrong side of the road" thing and the high-speed roundabouts, it was probably better for everyone that I wasn't behind the wheel of a car.

The natives I met were full of suggestions of things for me to see and do, and for the first few months, I wandered around like a tourist, dumbstruck with wonder. I'd gone from graduate student to Compton globetrotter overnight—my ass was jet-setting for real. I could hardly digest that this was my life. We didn't travel much when I was a kid; leisure wasn't exactly in the budget. Aside from an annual trip to visit my aunt in Fresno, we barely ever left LA. That was the main reason I wanted to go to college out of state—I was curious about what life would be like in a place like Oregon. All the brochures that came in the mail showed smiling faces frolicking in a lush, green landscape. The imagery appealed to me—we didn't have trees in South Central, not like that anyway.

Before I escaped to Oregon, my primary mode of travel had been through books. I read everything I could get my hands on: novels set in different times and places, biographies of the world's most influential leaders, nonfiction depicting key moments in history. Hell, I even read each volume in the encyclopedia set my mother acquired at a garage sale, from cover to cover. My quest for knowledge was insatiable, and I developed a particular fascination with history.

Studying abroad, I'd be able to visit landmarks that until now I'd only read about. And not only that, I stood at the gateway to Europe. Once I'd seen all there was to see here, places like Paris and Germany were just a train ride away. I'd be able to stand upon the site of the French Revolution, lay eyes on what was left of the Berlin Wall, and explore the ruins of the Roman Empire. This opportunity was a dream come true.

But first, I had to conquer London.

Chapter Five

Samantha

As I started my final year at UCSC, I was still adjusting to Damion's absence. It's funny how people become woven into the fabric of your life. Damion had been my safety blanket, and life without him was chilly at first. Lonely, for sure. But in time I got back into the routine of being an undergrad, emerged from my self-protective isolation, and tried to enjoy my last nine months of Stafford-subsidized freedom before being thrust into the real world.

Since I had no idea what I wanted to do post-college in terms of a career, the anticipation of graduation was filling me with a great deal of anxiety. Unless you wanted to pursue a doctoral degree or go to Law School, there wasn't exactly a clear next step for someone graduating with a Sociology degree. Of all the options batted around, graduate school seemed like the most logical, if only to buy myself more time to figure out what I wanted to be when I grew up. I was interested in educational reform, and possibly teaching, so perhaps a Master's degree and Teaching credential was the way to go. Assuming I could figure out a way to pay for it—grad school was expensive, and I'd already taken out about $20,000 in loans just to make it through my undergrad.

I could have really used Damion's counsel during these deliberations, since he had successfully navigated this particular series of decisions several years ago. Though we kept in touch via email, it just wasn't the same as our marathon sessions in the shade of Papa Wood. As we became immersed in our separate lives, the emails became less frequent and I realized what a crutch Damion had become. Not that I hadn't needed a crutch at the time, but when there's someone around who is so willing and able to take care of you, it's easy to forget how to take care of yourself. So after an initial period of missing Damion and feeling sorry for myself, I started to participate in my life again. I spent time with my girlfriends, signed up for a yoga class, and took every opportunity to indulge in my newfound love of live music.

I'd been spending a lot of time at Moe's Alley with my best friend, Faby. Moe's was a regular stop for many local and regional bands. I loved the dimly-lit club—one of the few public places I could go and still feel rather anonymous. Since the majority of patrons frequented the blues joint to see their favorite band, not hook up, the meat market vibe of your typical college club was absent. This was where true music lovers came to hear grown-folks music, and if a hook-up happened in the process, well, at least you could be certain you had one important thing in common.

Thanks to Tony, musicians were a weakness of mine. There was nothing sexier than an acoustic guitar in the hands of a soulful man. The first guy I dated post-Tony and post-Damion's departure was a bass player named Saul. Damn, was he hot. Hot enough to make me forget all about my boy hiatus and the irreparable damage men could cause. Saul played the bass in a local Ska band, and they had a standing, monthly gig at Moe's. Tall, dark, and handsome, Saul had strong arms and long, lean fingers that he put to serious work on the strings of that bass. Watching him onstage, I fantasized about what it would be like to have those hands and fingers working on me, the kind of sounds and melodies he might elicit from my lips. Like I said, I'm a sucker for musicians.

The first time I laid eyes on Saul, I hardly noticed him because I'd been at Moe's with Damion. Damion and I never paid much attention to the opposite sex when we had each other for company—there was no need. But it was a completely different story when I started going to Moe's with Faby and the girls. Meeting men was so easy. If the collective estrogen didn't magnetize them to our table, Faby would just go out and get one, like a mother lion bringing home food for her cubs.

"Girl, look at that hunk of chocolate over there. He's totally checking you out."

And the next thing you knew, she'd gotten us all invited backstage.

I'm not going to lie, I get the allure of groupie life. It's very exciting to be invited into that exclusive area behind the stage, where there are no rules. No joke—rock stars do whatever the fuck they like, many of them fully embracing that bad boy persona. They can also have any woman they want, so when they decide they want *you*, it's kind of a big deal. One for the books. One of those stories worth repeating long after the taste of his lips is gone.

Since Saul was a local boy, the typical rock star one-night-stand turned into an affair that spanned several months. He was actually a lot of fun, a total stoner who still lived at home and worked at his dad's construction company during the day. At 25, he didn't have much of a plan, but his humble aspirations never really bothered me—it's not like I was trying to *marry* the boy. Besides, he was *hot*. Smokin' hot will make a girl overlook a lot of things if there's an itch that needs to be scratched.

I stopped seeing him after three months when I realized that in true rock star/bad boy fashion, he had several other girls he was "making music" with. I wasn't hurt, or surprised even, but the discovery pretty much ruined the fantasy for me. We parted ways with no hard feelings and every once in a while I answer the phone when he rings me up at 2 a.m. Like I said, smokin' hot is good enough if all you're looking for is a bootie call.

After my Saul excursion, I had a fling with Karl, a drummer in a Hip Hop band out of Oakland. Karl was also smokin' hot, with bulging biceps, strong, tatted forearms, and a washboard stomach we all got to gaze upon when he removed his shirt midway through the second set. His glistening torso pulsed and flexed as he pounded out beats and rhythms on his drum, and it took me all of two seconds to acquiesce when he asked if I wanted to accompany him back to his hotel. The surprises kept coming when I discovered he was just as solid in his lower body as he was up top; he may be the most well-endowed man I've ever had the pleasure of laying down with. His rhythm and timing between the sheets was just as masterful as on stage, and to this day I can't hear a kick drum without thinking of him.

I attended his show in San Jose a few nights later, enjoyed my own private encore afterwards, then bid him happy trails as the band headed down to Southern California for the next leg of their tour. There was no drama since we both understood the temporary nature of these types of trysts. He promised to look me up if he was ever in the area, and I told him I looked forward to seeing him on MTV one day.

That year, I dated a disproportionate amount of musicians. The no-strings hook-up was my preferred mode of engagement because the last thing I wanted was for a man to stick around long enough for me to develop feelings for him. Yes, I had jumped back into the dating pool with both feet, but I was allergic to the idea of falling in *love*. I had no interest whatsoever in wandering down that road again, so the transient nature of musicians really suited where I was at in my life. We could come together out of mutual interest and need, party like rock stars, then resume business as usual. No permanent distractions, no broken hearts to take me out of commission. My kind of relationship—superficial and uncomplicated. Yet exciting enough to keep me from thinking too much about Tony... or Damion.

Chapter Six

Samantha

As graduation approached, I put the boys on the back burner and withdrew into a contemplative shell. I had lots on my mind as I became more and more preoccupied with the "what's next?" question. With two weeks left in my UCSC career, I was still absent a plan, leaving me no choice but to move back home.

It's hard to return to the nest after being on your own, and I was not happy about it. My mother, God bless her, had some boundary issues and was constantly meddling in the affairs of her kids. My sister, Megan, was almost thirty, making six figures as an editor at one of LA's hippest entertainment magazines, and still had to deal with a steady barrage of well-intentioned maternal criticism. I love my mom and all, but I was not trying to endure that level of scrutiny on a daily basis. My goal was to be out of her house in three months, tops.

Faby's parents were sending her to Europe as a graduation present, and for months Faby had been begging me to come along. As much as I wanted to join her on that adventure, there was no way I could swing something like that financially. I had *some* money saved up, but the flight alone was over a thousand dollars. Imagine my surprise when I opened the graduation card from my siblings and discovered they'd pooled their money to purchase a round-trip ticket for me, from LAX to London, on the same flight as Faby. I was stunned. My brothers and sister had made a dream come true, and I will never be able to repay them for their thoughtfulness and generosity.

I know, backpacking around Europe after college is such a cliché thing to do—if you're a rich girl, which Faby and I were not. But leave it to Faby to make not one, but two plane tickets appear. Faby was unstoppable once she set her mind to something, and she'd proven it once again. Her special skill was making things happen, and I felt pretty blessed to have been included in her latest manifestational exercise.

The plane ticket wasn't the biggest surprise I received on graduation day though. Oh no, the *biggest* surprise was the phone call from Tony, in the middle of my graduation party, informing me that not only was he in town, but that he desperately needed to see me.

The sound of his voice triggered an avalanche of dormant emotions. Reduced me to a puddle of want and need after I'd spent the past two years rebuilding the fortress around my heart in an attempt to repair the damage he'd done. But much to my frustration, the drawbridge to my fortress fell open at his command, allowing him to stroll back into the protected interior as if nothing had happened. Stupid, useless drawbridge.

Of course I went to meet him. Tony and I were like magnets whose sole purpose was to attach and bond. The man made me completely irrational. I snuck away and headed down to the beach, not knowing what to expect. I had no idea what he was going to say, or more importantly, how I'd respond. I'd be lying if I said I hadn't dreamed about this day many times, fantasized about how satisfying it would be to have him come crawling back, pledging his love and begging for forgiveness. Had that day finally arrived?

I made my way down the worn, dirt path to the edge of the cliff. My heart leapt when I spied him near the edge, staring across the sea, every bit as handsome as I remembered. He turned to face me and smiled. Past and present merged into one indistinguishable experience as then and now ceased to exist.

And just like that, it was back. That awful, yearning feeling. I hadn't felt this level of desperation since Tony exited my life, and had vowed to never succumb to that kind of emotional helplessness again. But reason had blown away with the ocean breeze. That had always been the problem—how completely out of control Tony made me feel.

"I had to see you," he said, fixing me with a penetrating glare. It was all I could do to stop myself from jumping into his arms.

I took a slow, steady breath. Must. Stay. In. Control. "Well, here I am."

"Yes, and all grown up. When I left, you were a girl, trying to find her place in the world. But you're all woman now. You wear it well."

It felt good to hear him say that. Though I was still figuring things out, I'd definitely come a long way since freshman year, and

Tony had played a major role in my transformation. Pain forces you to grow, and the maturity I now possessed was birthed out of my loss. I had learned the most important lesson of my life from Tony—that it was possible to come back from total devastation. That I had the strength to rebuild.

This epiphany was nearly as shocking as Tony's phone call had been. For the first time I was able to see the positive effect Tony's departure had on my life, and as the hurt and anger dissolved, I started to remember all the things I loved about him.

Then I noticed the thin, gold band encircling his ring finger. That piece of jewelry said more than any of the words coming out of his mouth.

"You married her?" I asked in disbelief. I was going to be sick.

Tony stammered through his response, something about how he was tricked, trapped, biggest mistake of his life—blah, blah, blah. And as he trotted out his parade of excuses, I was reminded of all the things I couldn't stand about him. He talked a good game, but at the end of the day he was weak and indecisive. He didn't fight for what he wanted. He didn't fight for *me*. And he should have. If he really, truly loved me, he *would* have.

We didn't get our happy ending, but it was good to get closure on the situation. To finally have answers to my lingering questions. To hear that he *had* loved me, that what I remembered as the "great love of my life" hadn't been a figment of my imagination. I needed that. But most important was the clarity I received about how that part of my life was over. I was the one walking away this time, and it felt good to end things on my own terms.

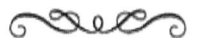

I didn't have much time to dwell on Tony's reappearance because Faby and I were fully immersed in vacation planning. And thank God—it was the perfect distraction from the emotional onslaught I'd just endured. As Faby and I pored over the maps and guidebooks, planning our itinerary, the raw emotional void and post-graduation anxiety was replaced by an exhilarating excitement about our coming adventure. This was a once in a lifetime opportunity and we wanted to do it right.

After purchasing ergonomic, trek-friendly backpacks from Outdoor World, we spent a lot of time trying to figure out how to fit everything we needed for three weeks abroad into *one* bag. Every guidebook and travel blog emphasized the importance of traveling light, and I was determined to try it. I just needed to convince Faby that she could live without seven pairs of shoes and an abundance of toiletries.

I held up the curling iron she'd placed in her "to pack" pile. "Really, Fab? You seriously want to carry this thing all over Europe?"

"What if we hit up a club or something? Not everyone was blessed with that *good hair*. Some of us have to work at it."

"Please, when you are up in the club in one of your famous mini dresses, the boys will be much too distracted by those shapely legs to worry about the lack of perfectly-formed ringlets." I tossed the curling iron onto the bed. "You are not going to need that."

After much agonizing, we finally pared our piles down to the bare essentials. I was bringing two pairs of pants, three pairs of shorts, two sundresses, one water-resistant sweatshirt (always plan for inclement weather), a hat, sandals and flip flops, a bathing suit and sarong (which could double as a beach towel), a dozen t-shirts and tank tops, and two weeks worth of underwear. That left just enough room for the critical toiletries, some books (and my journal), and a small first aid kit. Fully loaded, the pack weighed about 40 pounds, but I was able to carry it easily and comfortably. We were ready to roll.

Though we had a few must-visits (such as Amsterdam and Paris), Faby and I resisted the urge to do too much advance-planning. Part of the fun was making it up as we went along. Spontaneity isn't a luxury you get to enjoy when you're a full-time student, and we wanted to take full advantage of this rare gift. We'd move through the countries at our leisure, lingering longer in our favorite spots and skipping the unimpressive ones. There would be no rushing on this trip—no deadlines, no pressure. We were the masters of our destinies.

The first stop was a few days in London to visit Damion.

Chapter Seven

Damion

I'm not gonna lie—when I found out Samantha and Faby were coming to visit, I was juiced. Being a continent away from my family and friends was hard at times, and a care package from Cali was just what the doctor ordered. As their arrival approached, I worked overtime to finish up all my projects; I wanted to give them my full and undivided attention while they were here. Couldn't wait to show them around London, the city I'd been calling home for the past ten months.

I'd recently moved from the room I'd been renting on campus to a two-room flat in Brixton, a borough in Southeast London. I loved Brixton—the working class African-Caribbean community was rich with culture and flavor. Between Oregon and Santa Cruz, I'd been diversity-deprived for the better part of the last decade. It felt good to dwell amongst brown folks again.

Living in Brixton was also great for my research, as the city was the site of numerous race riots throughout the eighties and nineties. I'd been seeking out long-term residents for interviews, and the accounts I'd been hearing of those tumultuous times were fascinating. I could relate—I grew up in an inner city—much like Brixton—that had been ravaged by the social conditions brought upon by generations of poverty, systematic disenfranchisement, and institutionalized racism. With the exception of the chaos unleashed in the wake of the Rodney King verdict, there wasn't much raging against the machine going on in LA's inner cities, which I always found strange. Why weren't more people taking to the streets to protest the various injustices that were still very much a part of our everyday lives?

My life's work was dedicated to answering that question. By studying contemporary uprisings, I sought to identify the psychological factors and social circumstances that pushed an individual from passive, ambivalent observation to ACTION. Once I figured out the magic formula that spurred the masses to act, I'd use that knowledge to motivate my people to step onto the path toward empowerment. My generation was in need of its own Civil Rights Movement, and I was ready to light the match that sparked the flames of change.

I've always considered myself more Malcolm than Martin, but was feeling extra fired up these days thanks to this Persian woman named Taja, an outspoken, fire-breathing, force of nature. I first saw her at a coffee shop, arguing rather loudly with a French student about the inevitability of class warfare, a worn copy of Marx's *The Communist Manifesto* open on the table in front of her.

"Your complacency is exasperating!" she railed. "You are French! Your ancestors probably bled in the streets of Paris during the French Revolution. Yet you remain ignorant of your own history, your legacy."

"Choosing to focus on the future is not ignorance," the French boy shot back. "It's progressive."

"Any perspective that disregards the context in which it was created is flawed and hopelessly one-dimensional. Because your life is comfortable, and always has been, you are blind to your privilege, and those that sacrificed for the freedoms you now enjoy. Your comfort is not an excuse to withdraw from the struggle; you owe your life to the struggle!"

I was instantly attracted to the aggressive way she defended her positions and the intelligence that bolstered her arguments. She reduced that poor dude to a studdering, bumbling mess, clearly outmatched and embarrassed to have received such a thorough tongue-lashing, in front of witnesses no less. After his hasty retreat, I eagerly stepped up to the plate, excited to engage her beautiful mind. We spent the next six hours in ferocious debate before falling into bed for some equally passionate sex.

Taja and I started spending a lot of time together, staying up late into the night drinking wine and arguing about the most effective way to change the world. I thought I was a revolutionary, but Taja was on a whole other level. Some of the circles she ran in were pretty sketchy, especially this clique of anarchists who favored a literal interpretation of the phrase "by any means necessary." Needless to say, her 'Fight the Power' spirit was a huge turn-on. And the sex! *Man.* She fucked the same way she argued— like she was going to war. We were always battling to be on top, and she usually won (which I didn't mind, really—can't complain about *that* view). Then she'd sneak out in the middle of the night without a word. She *never* stayed the night. That was definitely a first.

Taja and I had a very mature understanding about the parameters of our relationship. Friendship was the foundation, and the sex an awesome, no-strings perk. I truly enjoyed Taja's company, and the affair satisfied many of my needs, but it wasn't *love*. There was still only one woman in my heart.

And she would be here in two days.

Chapter Eight

Samantha

The flight from LAX to London was no joke. We left at 11 a.m. California time, flew five hours to JFK, then another nine hours from New York to London. I tried to sleep on the plane, but it was impossible. I was too excited; the anticipation breeding a jittery restlessness, as if I'd consumed one too many cups of coffee. There was just so much to look forward to.

Damion met us at the airport, and when I caught a glimpse of his neatly twisted locks in the crowd, I couldn't resist running into his arms like we were long-separated lovers. I'd missed him so much—more than I cared to admit. Sometimes the best way to cope with someone's absence is to institute emotional distance, which I'd done. But seeing his face again made me feel all kinds of giddy. He scooped me up while Faby patiently waited her turn. Reunited and it felt *so* good.

"Aren't you two a sight for sore eyes." Damion beamed, his dark brown eyes glued to mine. "I haven't seen a familiar face since I left the States."

"I can't believe you've been here for almost a year," I said.

"I know. I may be here for a while, actually. They've offered me a teaching position in the History program."

"Really?" Faby asked, clearly impressed. "That's great, Damion. Congratulations!"

I congratulated him as well, but absorbed the news with mixed emotions. For some reason, the thought of Damion putting down roots over here made me sad.

We took the "Tube" back to his apartment in Brixton, which would serve as home base for the next couple of days. Damion insisted that we take his queen-sized futon, while he crashed on the tiny couch. I dropped my bag on the bed and collapsed. The clock on the bedside table read 12:22 p.m., but it was 4 a.m. in California and in my body. I hadn't slept a wink on the plane, and was ready for a nap.

"I know you guys are exhausted," Damion said, "but trust me, the best way to beat jet lag is to stay up. You need to reset your body clock. We'll stay local and keep it mellow, but you gotta stay awake. You can sleep in as late as you need to tomorrow."

"Who needs sleep?" Faby asked. She unpacked her toothbrush and headed toward the bathroom. "Give me a few minutes to freshen up and I'll be ready to hit the town."

I sat up and stretched. "I swear, if I had a fraction of her energy…"

Damion stood over me and rubbed my neck, which was tight from the long plane ride. "After you get some food and coffee in that belly, you'll be good to go. How do you feel about heading down to Electric Avenue for lunch?"

Faby emerged from the bathroom. "*The* Electric Avenue?"

"Yup," Damion replied. He pulled me to my feet and twirled me around. *"We gonna rock down to, Electric Avenue—"*

"And then we'll take it higher!" Faby and I joined in.

The Brixton Market, located on *the* Electric Avenue, spanned several blocks in central Brixton. The open-air marketplace, alive with culture and commerce, showcased food and goods from all over the world. You could get anything here, from fresh produce, fish, and meat to clothing, jewelry, and handbags.

We were greeted by the sound of bongo drums and pulsing reggae music as we approached. The diversity was stunning. Damion explained that about 25 percent of Brixton's population was from the Caribbean, one of the primary reasons he chose to live here. I could see the appeal. There's something comforting about being surrounded by other people of color, where your skin tone is the rule, not the exception. That certainly hadn't been the case in Santa Cruz, where Black students made up approximately three percent of the student body. All this brown skin was a real treat.

As we wandered down the street, checking out the various wares, Faby and I were overwhelmed by the vast selection of exotic foods. Rather than sit down to eat at a restaurant, we decided to snack and sample from a variety of street vendors until we couldn't eat anymore. We started at the Take Two Grill, where two Jamaican men were cooking jerk chicken in a kettle drum right there on the street. Then we sampled samosas from a little Pakistani café before moving on to try some West Indian food. We ended our food tour with gelato and coffee.

"Good lord, I feel like I just took my taste buds on a trip around the world," I said, savoring the rich, salt-caramel ice cream.

"This place is awesome, Damion," Faby added. "We are definitely getting our trip off to a great start."

"Glad you ladies are enjoying yourselves." He took a sip of espresso. "So, what kinds of stuff do you want to see in London—the touristy historical landmarks, or spots with more local flavor?"

"Both!" Faby and I answered in unison. We all laughed.

"I'm sure wherever you take us will be great," I said. "We just feel so lucky to have our own personal tour guide."

"Trust me, it is my pleasure. We can head into London tomorrow. How are you guys feeling? My ex-roommate is DJ-ing at a club here in Brixton tonight if you're up for it."

Clearly in possession of her second wind, Faby was quick to respond. "I'm ready to meet some hot British men. Is your ex-roommate hot?"

Damion laughed. "He seems to think so."

"Well then, hook it up, playa!"

After taking turns in the shower, we got dressed and headed out on the town. We started the night with dinner at Bamboula, a tasty restaurant serving up Caribbean food (I'd developed an insatiable craving for jerk chicken), then headed over to Dogstar, a popular nightclub in Brixton. The club was packed, but since Damion was friends with the DJ, we bypassed the line. We were escorted to our own private sofa adjacent to the DJ booth, which was perfect because after being awake for the past 42 hours, I didn't have the energy to stand, much less dance. But I did have a blast people-watching and getting my drink on while Damion took Faby out for several spins on the dance floor. I had no idea where she got all her energy.

Thankfully Faby started to lose steam around 11 p.m., so we called it a night. I was so exhausted I nodded off in the cab. The next time I opened my eyes, it was morning.

Chapter Nine

Damion

Yesterday was the best day I've had in London since I arrived. Being around Samantha felt so good—I don't know what kind of pheromones she was throwing off, but having her beside me enhanced my experience of everything. I referred to this altered state of reality as the "Samantha Effect." Her presence was hypnotic and distracting...just like I remembered. Which is why I had to leave the country. The girl had me jonesing like a junkie, and she was my drug of choice. I didn't even want to think about the withdrawal I'd have to suffer through when she left.

But while the girls were here, they were going to be treated like queens. After serving them breakfast in bed, we journeyed into the heart of London. The London Eye was our first stop. A Ferris wheel on steroids, the London Eye transported glass bulbs filled with awestruck tourists on an aerial sightseeing tour. We sipped champagne as the wheel made its leisurely revolution, staring across a landscape composed of palatial rooftops, centuries-old steeples, and the majestic River Thames winding through the city like a serpent. Since I was familiar with the city now, I was able to identify all the major landmarks in the distance. I made a mental note every time one of them expressed interest in a certain spot, and tried to work everything I could into our itinerary. After all, I aim to please.

Our spin on the wheel was like the appetizer that preceded a fantastic feast; it invigorated their palate and had them hungry for the next course. Next, we took a boat ride along the River Thames. Boat tours were a great way to see the city without having to do too much walking. The cruise also allowed us to get up close and personal with many of the scenic bridges that straddled the River Thames, each with a unique design and architecture. I pointed out the landmarks visible from the boat, such as Big Ben and the House of Parliament, while Sam and Faby snapped photos like giddy tourists.

After we disembarked, we cruised by Buckingham Palace, home to the royal family, admiring the gothic architecture prevalent throughout London along the way.

"I can't believe we're in a different effing country," Sam said.

"Shoot, I feel like we've time travelled to an entirely different era," Faby added. "Think about it—some of these buildings and churches have withstood two World wars. Gives a whole new meaning to the phrase 'if these walls could talk'."

"That's what I've appreciated most about living abroad," I said. "I've studied history my whole life, but it didn't land for me, until I got here, what a small space America occupies in the history of the world. But because it's all we know, we tend to privilege our worldview, not realizing how limited our perspective really is.

I thought my mind was open before, but now…" I chuckled. "Man, I didn't know shit."

"Look at you, Renaissance man," Faby teased. "But I agree with you. I feel sorry for people who don't get the chance to travel. There is so much to learn from spending time outside your comfort zone. Stuff they just can't teach you in school."

We picked up sandwiches for a picnic in St. Jame's Park. Though London was typically overcast this time of year, there wasn't a cloud in sight—yet another example of the Samantha Effect. We decided to relax for a while on the bank of St. Jame's lake, enjoying the gorgeous summer day.

"What's been your favorite part so far?" I asked, as we set up our picnic.

"Ooooh, that's a tough one," Faby said, clicking through the photos on her digital camera. "That boat ride was pretty awesome."

"I loved running around in Brixton," Samantha added. "I can't stop thinking about the food. This sandwich is so bland in comparison."

"I find a lot of London bland compared to Brixton," I replied, bursting with pride for my hood. "You definitely won't have to worry about blandness in Amsterdam though!"

Samantha's eyes lit up. "I know! I can't wait."

Imagining the look of glee on Samantha's face when she stumbled into her first pot shop, I couldn't help but laugh. "I bet you can't," I said with a wink. "I'm jealous—Amsterdam is the bomb. Great city. The only place outside of the UK that I've visited more than once."

"You should come with us!" Faby exclaimed.

Samantha and I both did a double-take—that was the *last* thing I expected her to say. "Really? I don't want to intrude on your little Thelma and Louise mission."

"You're not intruding—we love having you around! Isn't that right, Sam?"

Samantha cut her eyes at Faby. If we'd been sitting at a table, Samantha no doubt would have kicked her under it.

"Of course we'd love for you to come along," Samantha affirmed. "But I wouldn't want to take you away from your work…"

"There's nothing going on here that can't wait," I said quickly. "Count me in."

"Good, then it's settled," Faby said with a grin. "How about we spend two more days here, and head over to Amsterdam on Monday."

"Actually, there's an overnight ferry to the Netherlands that departs out of Harwich," I said. "We can spend the day sightseeing, hop on an eight o'clock ferry, and wake up Monday morning in Amsterdam."

"Now that's what I'm talking about," Faby said. "You are way better than any damn guidebook."

I couldn't repress the smile that broke out on my face. I'd been pouting internally all day at the thought of them leaving. What a tease to have them swoop through, remind me of what it felt like to be around family, to be around Sam, and then leave me behind with a soul full of longing. It never occurred to me that they might want me to tag along. What a wonderful development.

God bless the Samantha Effect.

Chapter Ten

Damion

We spent our last day at one of my favorite spots in town—Hyde Park—approximately 360 acres of green surrounding a large lake. We'd been going hard on the sightseeing front, trying to squeeze in as much as possible in the compressed timeframe, so it was nice to take a day to just relax. The weather was once again cooperating, and we were gifted with the perfect day for lounging outside. We set up camp on the bank of the Serpentine, a brilliant splash of blue amidst the lush, green landscape.

"Not exactly the Pogonip, but it'll do, huh?" I asked Sam.

She smiled. "I tend to place more emphasis on the company than the setting, but in this case, both are fantastic."

I couldn't agree more. Samantha and Faby had stripped down to shorts and bikini tops, and Samantha's caramel skin and the soft curve of her breasts beneath the pale, blue fabric provided me with some exceptional scenery. Was it possible that she was even more beautiful than I remembered? She was so relaxed now… the veil of distrust and pain that used to linger just below the surface of her smile had vanished. It really looked like she had finally started to heal.

She shocked the hell out of me when she told me that Tony had showed up at her graduation. I couldn't believe that he had the nerve to pop back into her life after all this time. But what really blew my mind was the news that Tony had actually *married* Angela.

Samantha relayed the story of their final encounter with a level of detachment I'd never seen where Tony was concerned. She didn't express any anger or disappointment about Tony's ill-advised nuptials, and appeared to be taking it all in stride. I wish I could say the same. I was steeped in guilt. I should have been there to talk some sense into him. Brothers don't let brothers marry the wrong people.

I'd only been in one serious relationship in my life, a 16-month stint with a girl named Kara who I met at the University of Oregon. Kara was what Tony referred to as a "trustafarian"—her parents were ridiculously wealthy and she spent her entire college career feeling guilty about, and rebelling against, her white privilege.

I'd never dated a white woman before, and was all kinds of sprung on that girl. I spent every dime I had showering her with gifts and whisking her away for romantic getaways. I'll admit, my young ass couldn't get enough of that fair-haired forbidden fruit, naively believing that racial harmony could be achieved by refusing to see color.

Even though I'd convinced myself that I was in love, Tony got a bad vibe from Kara the first and only time they met.

"Really, Dame? She doesn't strike me as your type…"

"Why, because she's white? Isn't *your* girlfriend white?"

"Come on, man, this isn't about skin color. I just never thought I'd see Mr. Black Power shacked up with a spoiled, rich girl."

I immediately jumped to Kara's defense. "She can't help where she came from any more than we can help our hood roots."

"And what does her daddy think about his baby girl's case of Jungle Fever?"

I frowned. "Shut up, man."

"What, she hasn't brought you home yet? Aren't y'all coming up on a year together?"

"Shut up, man."

But as offended as I was at the time, I knew his criticism came from a good place. And Tony ended up being right. Kara introduced me to her folks a few months later, and while they smiled politely at me across the dinner table, I didn't succeed in winning them over. Kara's father threatened to cut her off financially if she didn't end things with me, and she showed her true colors (pun intended) by bending to his will.

I was blindsided by the break-up and didn't take it well. I didn't care so much that I'd been dumped; I was more disturbed by the fact that I could spend so much time with someone and be so *wrong* about them. When Tony heard the news, instead of gloating or rubbing it in with "I told you so's," he drove up to Eugene from LA to take my heartbroken ass on a camping trip. After four days of fishing and male bonding on the Columbia River, I had put the whole traumatic affair into perspective. Damn, I missed those camping trips. And I missed Tony. As soon as Samantha and Faby headed back to the States, I was going to call Tony up and squash this beef once and for all.

"What are you thinking about?" Samantha asked, interrupting my trip down memory lane. Faby had wandered down to the small beach to wade in the water, providing me and Sam with a rare moment alone.

"Just making a mental list of the things I need to take care of before we leave this evening," I fibbed. It was probably best to steer the conversation *away* from Tony—no need to put a damper on this beautiful day.

"You're not having second thoughts about this impromptu trip, are you? The last thing I want to do is disrupt your routine."

"Routines are meant to be disrupted," I assured her. "Besides, I need this. As much fun as I'm having, it gets really lonely sometimes. Don't get me wrong—I've met some great people. But it's not the same as being around people who know you and love you."

"I know what you mean," Samantha said. "I've had a deficit in that area myself since you left." She paused, as if she was going to say something more, but thought better of it. "I'm really glad you're coming with us."

Me too, I thought.

Before we left, I took the girls to Speaker's Corner in the northeast corner of the park. Speaker's Corner was one big soapbox where folks gathered to debate everything from politics to football. I explained how Karl Marx and Marcus Garvey had once stood on this very corner, promoting their revolutionary ideals.

When we arrived, a very passionate Brit was on a rant about U.S. imperialism and our "irresponsible" war in Iraq. His verbal thrashing of President Bush drew thunderous applause from the onlookers. At one point, he invited any Americans in the crowd to speak up in defense of their country. I couldn't resist answering his call.

"First off, I must agree with you, sir. U.S. foreign policy of late has been reckless and destructive. Bush, who I did *not* vote for, is ill-equipped to lead and his actions have done irreparable damage to the U.S. and world economies. But it is wrong to judge an entire nation based on the actions of one man or the agenda of one political party. Not all Americans are selfish, spoiled, and 'ugly.' Elitism is abhorrent on any perpetrator, and stirring up anti-American sentiment makes you no better than Bush. Rather than promoting hatred, perhaps it might be more productive to reach out to your American brothers and sisters, who are also struggling, to form an international anti-establishment coalition."

More applause. The feisty Brit and I went a few more rounds before parting ways with a firm, respectful handshake. I could have debated this topic all afternoon—after all, these principles guided my research. But the girls and I had packing to do. The debauchery of Amsterdam was calling our name.

Chapter Eleven

Samantha

My cousin Reyna is a gypsy. When she was 29-years-old, she spearheaded a harassment suit against her employer, a Fortune 500 company that was turning a blind eye to a culture of sexism in the workplace. After recruiting several co-workers to join her lawsuit, the group emerged victorious and each received a six-figure settlement. To celebrate, Reyna took her unexpected windfall and hit the road, determined to see the world. She told her folks she'd be home when the money ran out. That was eight years ago.

Reyna had only returned to the States twice. The last time when her brother, my cousin Ronan, got married. I had just started school at UCSC, and remember clinging to her side all night, fascinated by the stories of her wild adventures across the globe. I admired her fearlessness, the way she refused to conform or settle. She was definitely taking the road less traveled, and I envied her. Hell, when I grew up, I wanted to *be* her.

"I've visited cities on several continents, each with a different vibe and way of life," Reyna said, after recounting the blissful month she'd spent working on a rice farm in Bali, Indonesia. "But there are some places that just resonate with my soul. Like I've lived and loved there in a previous life."

I'd never felt that way about a place before...until I got to Amsterdam. The city was completely different from anywhere I'd ever been, but for some reason I felt at home here. Charmed and enthralled, I was tempted to scrap the rest of the itinerary and post up in Amsterdam for the duration. Faby's response:

"All this weed is making you lazy. I'm cutting you off."

She may have had a point. We were smoking a *lot* of weed. Obscene amounts. We couldn't help it—Amsterdam was a pot smoker's heaven. After exiting the train station, we noticed the familiar smell of marijuana coming from... everywhere. Sure enough, the street was dotted with "coffee shops," cannabis-friendly establishments where you could purchase—and smoke—weed.

Damion led us down the narrow cobblestone lanes until we reached a coffee shop with reggae music booming out of the second story windows. From the outside, it looked like your run-of-the-mill café—patio seating, a chalkboard advertising specials, flyers for upcoming events taped to the window. But when Damion pushed open the door, a cloud of sweet-smelling smoke greeted us as patrons lounged about, puffing away without a care in the world.

Un-fucking-real.

We approached the counter and my mouth fell open. Canisters of crystally-green buds lined the bar, a glorious display. As long as you were over the age of eighteen, you could partake—no special card needed, no forms to fill out. No hassle or judgment. And you could smoke right there! They even had pipes and vaporizers you could borrow! It was the most convenient thing ever!

I read the labels on the jars—White Widow, Purple Haze, Amnesia, Blueberry. These were strains I'd only read about in *High Times*. You could purchase weed by the gram, or in pre-rolled joints (with tobacco or without). They also had hash, wax, and an impressive selection of edibles. There was almost *too* much choice.

"Okay, I am officially overstimulated," I confessed. "What's the difference between an indica and a sativa?"

The petite budtender smiled and said, in perfectly good English, "Primarily the growing technique—indoor vs. outdoor. Sativa, which is grown outdoors, is more of a mind high, while an indica affects the body, leaving you relaxed and lethargic."

"What do you recommend?" Damion asked.

"It really depends on the effect you're seeking. And your budget."

The budtender gave us an overview of the store's most popular strains, and our happy trio decided to go with the Silver Haze, a sativa. After all, we had a whole day of sightseeing ahead of us. After adding some pastries and tea to our order, we borrowed the vaporizer and found a comfy couch to chill on.

Folks who are not career stoners (*cannabaseurs*, if you will) probably can't tell the difference between Mexicali bammer and *really* good weed. Back in Santa Cruz, I'd been blessed with access to a lot of excellent pot; I knew what the good stuff was supposed to look and smell like. But the store-bought nug I held between my fingers was something else. This thing had obviously been cultivated with love—I could probably get high off the scent alone. But the aroma wasn't its only supersized feature. The potency was off the chain. We only needed a few puffs each and we were flying high, tripping out on our strange, new surroundings.

Though it was the middle of the day on a Monday, there were a decent amount of people lazing around—most of them tourists. The vibe was relaxed and friendly, everyone chilled out and having a mellow time. Two older men were immersed in an intense game of chess in the corner. Several people were reading, a few writing, and others engaged in lively conversation. But everyone was smoking, casual and carefree, like it was the most normal thing in the world.

I fucking *loved* this town.

We lounged on that couch for over an hour, alternating between blissful contentment and bursts of uncontrollable laughter. "I never, ever want to leave," I mused, biting into the most amazing chocolate croissant I'd ever tasted.

"It is ridiculous how comfortable these pillows are," Damion said, his long legs stretched underneath the polished, oak coffee table. "Think they'll let us borrow a few cushions for the afternoon?"

"Doubtful," I replied.

He glanced around the room. "There's a ton of pillows in here. They probably wouldn't even notice if a couple went missing for a few hours."

Convinced that it was essential these pillows accompany us on our mission, Damion began strategizing about how to make off with a cushion or two.

"I've got it!" he exclaimed excitedly, pulling us into a conspiratorial huddle. "Sam and I will create a distraction… maybe stage a lover's quarrel or something. Then Fab, while the waitress is dealing with us, tuck a few under your shirt, creating a faux womb, and slip out. I bet they won't even notice you!"

"Oh hell no," Faby replied. "I'm not trying to get thrown into a Dutch prison so you can have something soft and squishy to rest your ass on."

We busted up laughing.

Yes, it was definitely silly season in Amsterdam.

After rolling a few joints for the road, we headed over to our hostel to see if we could check in early, or at the very least, store our bags. The Winston St. Christopher's, right in the heart of the Red Light District, was going to be home for the next few days.

Hostels are the way to go if you're traveling on a tight budget. As little as 20 euro a night can get you a bed in a single-sex or mixed dorm. Sure you have to share a bathroom, and there isn't much privacy, but the reality is, if you're traveling right, you don't spend very much time in your room. All you really need is a place to lay your head at the end of the night and a hostel does the trick. Quite nicely.

We booked an eight-bed, mixed dorm room for two nights. Our dorm mates included a couple in their forties from New Zealand, a solo male traveler from Germany en route to Denmark, and two Japanese-American sisters from Chicago celebrating the older sister's recent divorce.

You meet the most interesting folks in hostels. Imagine a building that collects individuals in the midst of some epic adventure or journey. People who are searching, running, or fiercely dedicated to the act of *living*. I found it comforting to meet all these new people and realize I wasn't the only one in transit; I wasn't the only person experiencing an existential crisis. I wasn't *alone*. On the contrary, I was amongst kindred spirits at the Winston St. Christopher's, and as we made the acquaintance of these transitory beings, I got caught up in the swirl of stories… the quests… the passion for life.

"Deciding to leave my husband was one of the most difficult decisions I've ever had to make," Yoshi, the divorcee, explained as we shared a joint on the back patio. "He was a good man. But we got married so young—I was only nineteen when I became his wife. I hadn't even figured out who I was yet."

"I can't even imagine," I said. "I can barely deal with my own needs, much less those of another person."

"Seriously," Faby added. "Marriage is such a serious commitment. There are so many things I want to do before I settle down."

"Exactly," Yoshi said. "I have goals and dreams beyond being a wife and mother, and I am finally free to pursue them. I have no idea where to start, but the freedom to choose is something so many women take for granted."

I was inspired by Yoshi's story. She had hit the reset button on her life trajectory and, like me, was moving forward with a clean slate and no idea what the future held. But instead of letting the uncertainty breed anxiety, she was viewing this new phase as an adventure.

That was the attitude *I* needed to cultivate.

Yoshi and her sister recommended a canal cruise operated out of "Boom Chicago," a comedy club down in Leidesplein. In addition to being one of the more affordable cruises, you were also allowed to drink and smoke on board. Sharing a joint while cruising the canals sounded like a great way to spend the afternoon, so off to Leidesplein we went.

Chapter Twelve

Samantha

Amsterdam is ridiculously picturesque, much more so than London in my opinion. Lovely, brick architecture lines the charming, cobblestone streets, with most roads bisected by a system of canals. Think Greenwich Village meets Venice, Italy. With the exception of the bicycles whizzing by (Amsterdam's preferred mode of transportation) the pace of life was slowed way down. Everyone was so chill here, though I'd expect nothing less from a city forward-thinking enough to decriminalize marijuana.

The canal cruise run by Boom Chicago was a great idea. Not only did we get to experience a leisurely afternoon floating along the lazy rivers, but our tour guide, one of the regular comedians at Boom Chicago, had us rolling with his hilarious anecdotes and commentary on Dutch culture. He provided the perfect introduction to the essence of Dutch Life.

"Here in the Netherlands," he explained, "we have an expression, *gezellig*. There is no exact translation in English, but it means, roughly, 'cozy, pleasant, and inviting.' A space or place where good things happen. Everything we do is *gezellig*. We seek pleasure. We delight in connection and conversation. We enjoy our food, our wine, our time. We do not hurry through things the way some cultures do."

He didn't specifically call out the Americans on the boat, but we knew who he was talking about. The pursuit of the almighty dollar was the centerpiece of capitalist American culture, and leisure, which eroded productivity, was not exactly a national priority in the U.S. the way it was in Europe.

After our 75-minute cruise, we disembarked and wandered through the Jordaan district on our way back to the hostel. Exploring the city on foot was a whole other experience, the narrow streets a chaotic swarm of pedestrians, bicycles, scooters, trams, and the occasional car. I couldn't quite figure out how yielding and right of way worked around here—people seemed to just turn or stop wherever they pleased, jaywalking whenever they needed to cross the street. Following a smoke break over a bowl of White Widow (which got us super-duper high), we exited onto the Singel, one of the busier thoroughfares, approaching our street crossing like we were in a real life game of Frogger.

"Okay, here we go," Faby said, glancing up the road. "Don't die!" And into the street she went with a subtle hop.

Or maybe I imagined the hop. Anyway…

What I came to understand about the craziness that was your typical Amsterdam intersection is that what appeared to an outsider as chaos was really a communal surrendering to the concept of flow. You can tell the locals from the tourists just by the way they approach an intersection. A tourist, whether on foot or on bike, will stop and wait at an intersection for a break in traffic, wearing a mask of trepidation as the cyclists zoom by. Natives, however, just pull into traffic and trust that whoever is coming will do their part not to hit them. On the surface what looked, well, suicidal, was really just evidence of relaxed, unwavering faith.

I witnessed this over and over again on the streets of Amsterdam until I finally decided to try it for myself. And so began my experiment of moving through each day with unfiltered trust, faith, and a complete lack of fear.

The happy hour at our hostel served 2-for-1 drinks until 11 p.m., so after getting a healthy buzz on, we headed out to explore the infamous Red Light District. Night had fallen, but the number of people on the streets had tripled. I soon understood why. The Red Light District was like Disneyland for freaks, fetishists, and deviants. Vegas on steroids. Sex, like the smell of marijuana, was everywhere. The shelves in the souvenir shops were stocked with penis paraphernalia, and the sex shops boasted a mind-blowing variety of sex toys. (Personally, I don't see why anyone would want a foot-long dildo, but I digress…) Point is, when it came to sex, you could find whatever tickled your fancy with ease. Including women.

Ever since I saw the movie *Dangerous Beauty* in high school, I've been fascinated with sex workers, from the courtesans who serviced the Kings of England and France, to the Japanese geishas, to the prostitutes and strippers in the present day. History is filled with tales of women who rose to positions of prominence and influence by playing to man's Achilles heel—his desire. To many, the wielding of sex as a weapon is nothing more than whoring, but the use of female sexuality as power has always intrigued me. Several of my papers at UCSC centered around this theme. After all, if we were going to be objectified by men regardless, why not use it to our advantage?

And now to be here in Amsterdam, where prostitution was actually legal! Talk about a unique vantage point. The narrow alleys in the Red Light District were lined with glass doors and windows displaying scantily-clad, flesh and blood mannequins marketing their "services" to potential customers… and there were plenty of customers milling about.

I couldn't believe how efficient it all was. Patrons browsed and shopped until they found something they liked, then approached the door to negotiate a price. Once someone was allowed entry, the curtain came down. This happened over and over, in plain view of the tourists and passerbys. After about 15-20 minutes, the satisfied customer would emerge. I watched all types of men complete these transactions—young, old, of all races and colors, and yes, even some wearing wedding bands. The young boys in town on stag parties were extra entertaining as they tended to bound out of the doors wearing big, cheesy smiles, bombarded by high fives, back slaps, and a barrage of questions from their friends. How many boys had lost their virginity here in the Red Light District?

"This is fascinating," I said, resisting the urge to take notes. I felt like I was studying some strange species, man in his primal element.

"It's sad," Faby said, as a group of drunk British boys heckled a heavyset, dark-skinned prostitute in her fifties. "To feel like you have no choice but to sell your body."

"I don't know, Fab, I don't see victims posturing behind that glass," I countered. "It's just sex, which is not shrouded in sin and taboo here the way it is in the States. Yes, the female body is a commodity in this free-market zone, but these women are not mere objects—they are in charge here."

"If you say so."

"No, seriously. Think about it. They set the fees and make the rules. If you are unwilling to play by their rules, you are denied access. These women are commanding a very decent wage for the services they provide. I say, more power to them."

We turned the corner and the usual flow of Amsterdam foot traffic came to a halt. A large group of people were lined up to enter an establishment called Casa Rosso.

"I wonder what's going on in there," Damion said.

"Oh, that's a live sex show," Faby said. "I saw a coupon for it in the brochure I picked up at Boom Chicago." She rummaged through her bag to retrieve the pamphlet. "Here it is—free drink with price of admission."

Damion glanced up the street. "Must be some show—that's quite a line."

"We should check it out," Faby said. "It's supposed to be really good. And we have a coupon."

I had to admit, I was more than a little curious. I'd been to a strip club in Los Gatos once with my friend Gabe, and left totally unimpressed. How would it compare to the scene here in

Amsterdam, the land where, sexually, anything goes?

Ninety minutes later, we emerged from the theater in an altered state of consciousness. Turns out, the term "live sex show" is quite literal. In front of a room full of people, an assortment of couples performed various sex acts (choreographed to music!) on a rotating bed at center stage.

"I can't believe we just watched strangers have sex for an hour," I said, still consumed by the erotic imagery being enacted a mere ten feet from my seat.

"An hour and a half," Damion corrected, a glazed look in his eyes. "I need a cold shower."

"I need a cigarette," I added.

"Fuck that," Faby proclaimed. "I need to get *laid.*"

Chapter Thirteen

Samantha

On day two in Amsterdam, we headed back to the picturesque Jordaan for breakfast and another round of wandering and coffee shop hopping. The prevalence of these pot shops really tripped me out. Each one had a different vibe, with a unique décor, musical selection, and menu. I was determined to check out as many as possible, my own personal comparative study.

Our funds were limited, so instead of shelling out cash for museums and other touristy attractions, we adopted a more anthropological approach to traveling. Each country was a little world, a microcosm of people, languages, cultures, and customs. In four days I'd already gotten a sampling of historic London and inner-city, working class Britain. Now I was getting a taste of Amsterdam, which appeared to be the hippie haven of the continent, a lively, tolerant, multicultural land. I couldn't imagine what France and Germany might be like, assuming I was able to tear myself away from the Netherlands.

"I want to move here," I repeated for the fourth time since we'd arrived. I was in love with all these damn canals. Almost every street was bordered by a canal, and it was so soothing to be surrounded by all this water. I've always had a thing about water. Whether it was the rhythmic crash of waves against the shore or the quiet stillness of a mountain lake, water had a calming effect on me. A surefire catalyst for a meditative trance.

As the day progressed, all that water (and ridiculously potent weed) put me in a mood. I often became antisocial when I smoked, turning inward to ponder the mysteries of life in quiet contemplation. But the weed here had me on a whole other level in regard to internal deliberations. Every lingering question about my future cycled through my mind as I zoned in and out of conversation with my companions. This trip to Europe had succeeded in masking my post-graduation anxiety, but eventually I would have to head back to California and start a life. Doing something. I was truly at a crossroads... several of them... more like an asterisk really... and I had no idea what I was supposed to do with myself.

Up to this point, my path had been pretty much laid out for me. Go to high school. Graduate. Go to college. Graduate. I'd achieved those milestones easily, because I've always been good at following directions and completing tasks, even with all the ways I'd been emotionally hijacked along the way. That was my special skill—the ability to power through and get things done once a task had been identified.

What I *wasn't* particularly good at was making decisions in the absence of a clear path. Too much choice overwhelmed me.

It's a lot of pressure knowing that whatever decision you make, whatever the outcome, you will have no one to blame but yourself. But as Yoshi had pointed out, the freedom to choose was a gift. Just had to make sure I didn't squander it.

We were posted up at La Tertulia, my new favorite coffee shop in the Jordaan district, smoking and people-watching. My gaze was fixed on a young couple melded into a passionate embrace on the bridge when I saw him in my peripheral vision—a brown-skinned, curly-haired man who looked an awful lot like Tony.

Damn that Amsterdam weed. Now it had me hallucinating.

I saw Tony a lot actually. Always at a distance, or on the periphery, but he did appear from time to time at the most inconvenient moments. Usually when I was in the company of another man. I'd be going about my business, having a lovely time, when I'd catch a glimpse of him. He haunted me. Though I was determined to keep Tony in the *past*, I've come to accept these visitations as normal. Some people just stick around, I guess. The flipside of love they never tell you about—it does last forever, if only to torture you.

The man/mirage on the bicycle turned a corner, freeing me from my trance. It wasn't him; it couldn't have been him. But the effect was the same—the visage brought me back to that achy place. As I stared across the rippled water, I couldn't help but think about how much Tony would have loved Amsterdam. We had talked about coming here together, one of many cities on our couple's bucket list. A list we were supposed to have a lifetime to tackle. He would have been right at home amongst the progressive inhabitants of this charming town. I could see him playing an acoustic set at a local café, or baking edibles for one of the many coffee shops. Tony definitely knew his way around the kitchen. I'll never forget the time he made me *adobo* from scratch…

Snap OUT of it, Samantha!

Yeah, the memory lane thing was not productive. Maybe it *is* time to lay off the weed.

I turned my attention to Damion. He'd always been good at keeping my mind off Tony, even though he represented the only tangible link I had to him. And while it was great having Damion on this adventure with us, something was starting to change. His overtures had taken on a flirtatious tone, and I could feel myself starting to reciprocate. If we're being completely honest, a mutual attraction had always been there, just below the surface. I mean, what's not to love—Damion's the *perfect* guy. Kind, honest, chivalrous. A true gentleman and the closest I've come to a prince in real life. But it just feels so wrong! Right, but wrong! Damion and Tony were like brothers, and even though Tony was no longer in the picture, hooking up with Damion felt like such a betrayal. Incestuous, even. How could a relationship between us possibly work out?

There was no mistaking the intimacy developing between us. Damion would casually slip his arm around my waist as we walked down the street or rest his hand on the small of my back as we rode the train. It was nice and innocent so far, but what if he made a move? How could I let him down without damaging our friendship? Was inviting him to join us a mistake? Should we politely send him back to London?

I posed this question to Faby the next time we had a moment alone. Much to my surprise, she had no desire to send Damion packing.

"Why would you want to do that?" she asked. "It has been great having him with us. He knows so much about navigating the landscape—we're saving a ton of time and money on account of his tips."

"I know. I guess I'm just concerned that he may be getting a little…attached."

Faby rolled her eyes. "Please, you two have been doing this dance for years. It's what you do."

"What the hell is that supposed to mean?"

"You know, acting like a couple without any of the benefits. I think you should just fuck and get it over with. Release some of that tension. Then you'll know once and for all which category he falls into."

"That is a terrible idea," I said, shaking my head.

"Why? I thought it was *just sex*," she mocked. "What makes Damion any different from all the other guys?"

I chewed on my lower lip, something I did during moments of extreme discomfort. "He just is."

"Well, maybe *that's* something worth exploring."

I quickly exited the conversation. Faby's advice was not helping.

Chapter Fourteen

Damion

After lunch, Samantha slipped into one of her trademark "funks." She was prone to brooding, and those close to her knew that the occasional dark cloud of depression came with the territory. But for it to show up here in *Amsterdam* of all places? Yesterday she had gone on and on about how this was her favorite place on the planet and the happiest she'd ever been. Words she meant, I could tell. But somewhere along the way a switch had been flipped and she had devolved into inexplicable sulking.

Ironically, Samantha reminded me of Tony when she was in this mood. He was also predisposed to long bouts of deep, intense thought and an impenetrable and slightly irrational melancholy. Which is why I knew exactly how to deal with Samantha's temperament shifts. Like Tony, if I left her alone and didn't aggravate her condition, it would eventually pass. But that could take days, and we simply didn't have that kind of time. This situation called for an immediate intervention. I was not about to sit back and let Samantha pout her way through Europe.

"What do you guys want to do after we finish gawking at the hookers?" I asked. We'd been wandering around the Red Light District for over an hour, as some of the most beautiful women I'd ever seen posed and coveted suitors through the glass. Samantha, a staunch advocate for sexual liberation and the rights of sex workers, was transfixed by the scenes unfolding before her eyes.

Faby clutched a paper cone filled with mayonnaise-slathered French fries, a Dutch staple. "I'm down for whatever," she said. "How about you, Sam? Any requests?"

"I'd love to interview one of the prostitutes," Samantha said out of nowhere. "Do you think I could pay someone to just… talk?"

Faby and I both whipped our heads in her direction.

"What?" Samantha asked. "Okay, I guess I would be open to more than just talking… That sex show definitely kicked my libido into gear."

I'm not gonna lie, I developed a rather inappropriate erection when she let that one fly.

"Samantha, you are not seriously trying to solicit a freakin' prostitute," Faby scolded. "Have you lost your mind?"

"My mind is just fine," Samantha shot back. "Aren't we here to have *experiences*?"

While I originally thought Samantha was kidding, I could see now that she was dead serious. Samantha and Faby both turned to me. Apparently I held the tiebreaking vote.

Samantha's proposition was out there, but if it succeeded in snapping her out of this damn funk, it would be worth it.

"Well, I mean, I can see the draw from a research perspective…" I began.

"Good, then it's settled," Samantha interjected. She marched off down the street, a woman on a mission.

Faby fixed me with a stern look, the one Latina mothers use to express their disapproval and disappointment. "Thanks a lot," she said, hurrying after Sam.

Samantha stopped at the corner as Faby rattled on about what a terrible idea this was. Her protests fell on deaf ears.

"I guess the next step is to find one you like," I said, calling Samantha's bluff. I was curious to see if she would actually go through with it.

"I already know which one I want," Samantha replied, a naughty flicker in her eyes. "Busty Latina. Red corset. She's in the alley near Oudekerksplein."

And with that she was off, leaving me and Faby no choice but to follow.

Chapter Fifteen

Samantha

Yes, you read it here. I spent intimate time with a prostitute in the Red Light District and enjoyed every sinful minute of it.

Thirty, to be exact. Thirty lovely minutes, though it felt like much longer.

It may seem strange that I would seek out such a seedy experience. What can I say—I was beyond intrigued by these sultry ladies behind the glass. As I watched them, I longed to know their stories, the circumstances that led them to this line of work. I'd spent my college career writing about these women, but had never actually spoken to one. This was an opportunity I couldn't pass up. Besides, I needed a distraction. I was not about to let the ghost of relationships past ruin my vacation.

My courtesan's name was Mariana, a caramel-kissed Latina with large breasts, a tiny waist, and full, womanly hips. A perfect figure 8, and heavy on the curves. She was the kind of gorgeous you'd find in a hip-hop video—bronze and thick in all the right places. It blew my mind that men could actually pay to have sex with such a stunning specimen—she was way out of *everyone's* league.

English was not Mariana's first language, and her words were coated in a thick accent that I would later learn was Colombian. When I approached her, she assumed I wanted to arrange a threesome for me, her, and Damion. When I told her that I wanted to pay to "just talk," she was skeptical, but accommodating. We agreed on forty Euro for thirty minutes of conversation—quite a bargain for a prostitute of this caliber. I sent Damion and Faby away, even though Faby was still loudly voicing her disapproval as Damion escorted her down the street.

"We'll be back," he called.

I waved and shut the door.

Mariana let the curtain down on the front window and joined me in a small back room that contained a bed, table, and two chairs. She gestured for me to take a seat and I opted for the chair. How many men had she serviced on that bed?

This was the first question that flew out of my mouth once our interview began.

"I don't keep count," Mariana said, crossing her long, shapely legs. "But during a good week, I may see 50-60 men. Many are regular customers though; not all strangers."

I did the math in my head—at fifty Euro per customer, that was about 2500 Euro *a week*. "Which do you prefer—regulars or strangers?"

"It is nice to be with someone familiar, as you have a, how do you say it, routine? But it is also nice to see new people, the tourists. I charge them more." She smiled.

"Is there anything you don't do?"

"Oh, there is much I don't do. I don't do the anal." She made a face. "I don't allow anyone to tie me up."

"Do you get that request a lot?"

"Every now and then. I have heard it all."

"Do you always use condoms?"

"Always."

"Even when you give blow jobs?"

"Yes. I am allergic to the taste of semen. Makes me bite."

She clamped her teeth together to demonstrate and we both laughed. Nice to see she still had a sense of humor.

Mariana noticed me admiring her cleavage. "Do you want to touch them?"

I blushed. "Is... is that included?"

She smiled and gestured for me to join her on the bed. "I will not offer if it is not *included*. Agree?"

I nodded and sat down. She removed her corset and placed my hands on her breasts. They were soft, warm, and surprisingly perky given their size. "Are these real?" I asked.

She laughed. "Yes."

I hadn't been blessed with big boobs and had never felt anything bigger than my modest A-cup. Mariana's nipples hardened beneath my palms as I squeezed and massaged her supple mounds.

"Can I touch you?" she asked.

I turned her question around in my head. This whole detour was wildly erotic. "You don't have to," I said, even though in this case, no kinda meant yes.

Thankfully, she figured as much. God bless the woman's intuition. She unbuttoned my blouse and gently fondled my nipples.

We lay back on the bed as she covered my exposed torso with kisses. "What else would you like to ask me?" she asked.

I could feel moisture accumulating down below. Her touch was so gentle... Even though we didn't have much time, she didn't force or rush the way many men do. "Oh, uh..." I sighed as her tongue flicked against my erect nipple. "How often do you actually reach orgasm with one of your clients?"

"It is rare, but also not important. This is about the customer's pleasure, not mine. Besides, it takes a bit longer than fifteen minutes for me to orgasm when I make love."

"So you draw a distinction, between having sex and making love?"

"Yes. This is work. There is no intimacy. I save that for my boyfriend."

"Oh, so you have a boyfriend?"

She frowned and shook her head. "Not right now. It is hard for men to accept what I do unless they are also in the business. But if they can't take care of me and my daughter, I have to work. She is my first priority."

"How old is your daughter?"

"Eleven."

"Does she know what you do?"

"Not yet, but I will need to have the talk with her soon. I'm not ashamed of what I do, but she is still a child in my eyes."

I rolled her nipple between my fingers. This was actually kind of fun. The female body was so beautiful. "What would you say if she wanted to do this kind of work? Would you allow it?"

"Oh no. I work very hard so she will have opportunities. I don't ever want her to struggle like this. I do this so that she will have a better life."

"I understand."

Striking such a personal chord must have made Mariana uncomfortable because she switched gears and started outlining some of the business aspects of her occupation. She explained the cost and process for renting the windows, and the expectations the government had for sex workers to register themselves and pay taxes on their income. As with anything, the legalization of prostitution in 2000 had both positive and negative impacts on the lives of Amsterdam prostitutes, but Mariana seemed to focus more on the positives, such as increased safety measures and unlimited access to STD testing.

And the entire time she spoke, she continued to stroke and fondle me.

As I lay half naked on the bed, in her arms, I found myself strangely at ease with my surroundings and the situation I found myself in. Not to mention totally turned on.

"What else would you like to know?" Mariana asked. We had burned through half of our allotted time together.

"Actually," I began, feeling rather bold, "I'm curious to see if I can bring you to orgasm in fifteen minutes…"

After bidding Mariana goodbye, I slipped into the alley. I was greeted by several raised eyebrows, as folks must not be used to seeing women emerge from behind those debaucherous doors.

"So, how was it?" Damion asked, his eyes wide.

I could not stop smiling. "What can I say—I kissed a girl… and I liked it."

Chapter Sixteen

Damion

Though Samantha would have preferred to stay in Amsterdam a while longer, it was time to move on. Faby was anxious to get to Paris, home to some of the world's most renowned art and architecture.

I'd gotten to know Faby on a whole other level the past few days. When you're with someone 24-7, the core of their character reveals itself quickly. Faby actually had a lot going on in that pretty little head of hers, and I realized I'd misjudged her on a number of fronts. For example, I'd always thought she was Type A and controlling—and not in a good way. But what I came to understand and appreciate was that Faby's obsession with having everything "just right" was fueled by a fierce ambition. Unlike Samantha, Faby knew exactly what she wanted to do with her life and was making her way toward that goal with calculated precision.

"Now that I've got my Art History degree taken care of, the next step education-wise is to get my Master's in Interior Design," Faby explained. "The program I'm interested in is very competitive, so before I apply I'm going to take a year to beef up my résumé. I have a nine-month internship with one of LA's top architects waiting for me when I return from Europe."

I was impressed. "Wow—how'd you land that gig?"

"Good ole fashioned networking," she said with a smile. "I laid out my plans and goals for my advisor at UCSC, and she put me in touch with one of her contacts in LA. I totally nailed my interview and was hired on the spot. The firm is even underwriting part of this trip so I can study various architectural styles up close, and I fully intend to get them to pay for my Master's as well."

Faby's confidence and drive were something else—she was blazing a bright trail toward a career fully in line with her passion. Quite the contrast to Samantha's tortured ambivalence. But Faby was the exception, not the norm—something I tried to remind Samantha of whenever she started to get down on herself for not having her next five moves mapped out. Unless you were continuing on to Grad School, it was common for recent college grads to enter some sort of occupational limbo as they tried to figure out the next step. I actually admired Sam's process—it took a lot of guts to linger in uncertainty because you refused to settle. Samantha didn't just want a job—she was trying to find a calling. She was asking herself tough questions, questions more people should ask before they chart a course through life. What makes me happy? How can I best give back to the world? What is my purpose here on this planet? Those were important, worthwhile questions. Samantha just needed to trust that the answers would come.

Her mood had improved after her session with Mariana, but she was still pensive and withdrawn. However, what Samantha lacked in overt enthusiasm, Faby more than made up for. During our three-hour train ride from Amsterdam to Paris, Faby gave me a spirited overview of the history of architecture in France. The girl was speaking my language as she showed me how history could actually be mapped through the structures of the times. Who knew so many practical, as well as aesthetic, considerations went into designing a building? Fascinating stuff. I was really enjoying Faby's company; there is nothing sexier on a woman than passion coupled with extreme intelligence.

Faby listed all the sights she hoped to see during our time in Paris. Her itinerary was ambitious, but I had no doubt Faby would be able to cover all that ground. She was, after all, on a mission.

Thanks to Faby's hook-ups, we didn't have to stay in a hostel during our time in Paris. Her firm had been contracted to renovate one of the hotels near the Lourve, and Faby had a comped room for the duration of her stay. This was definitely a treat, as the place was *très* fancy. Polished marble floors covered the lobby and crystal chandeliers dripped from the ceilings, their sparkly tendrils glistening in the light. The walls were streaked with gold. No, really, I wouldn't be surprised if there was *actual gold* mixed into the paint. This place was *that* fancy.

Our room was small (as most hotel rooms in Europe are), but we were happy to have a bathroom we didn't have to share with thirty other people. The first thing we did after checking in was take turns in the shower.

Faby went first, which gave Samantha and I some alone time. She sat cross-legged on one of the twin beds, staring out the window at the boulevard below.

"Thinking about Mariana?" I teased.

"No… just marveling at how insane it is that I'm here in Paris. This is so surreal."

"Yeah, I hear you on that one." I sat down beside her. "The last thing I thought I'd be doing this summer is backpacking around Europe with two gorgeous women. I am one lucky guy."

"We're the lucky ones. You're like our own personal bodyguard. I love having you around to protect us."

I smiled. "Well, I love being around you, period. I really missed you, Sam."

"I missed you, too." She wrapped her arms around my waist. "More than you know."

"Don't stop there," I said. "I live to hear beautiful women sing my praises."

Instead of a barrage of compliments, I got a pillow upside the head.

"Oh, really?" I snatched the pillow out of her hand and tackled her. "I protect you from thieves and bar trolls and this is the thanks I get?" I tickled her sides as she tried to wriggle away.

"No, fair," she gasped. "You know how ticklish I am!"

After a few minutes of playful wrestling, I had her pinned beneath me. Damn, I wanted to kiss her. I had the urge about twenty times a day, but something always stopped me. But on this bed, in a hotel room in the middle of Paris, the urge was irresistible…

The shower cut off. Faby would be re-entering the space in a few minutes and the moment was lost.

Samantha freed herself from my grasp as Faby emerged from the bathroom, so fresh and so clean.

"All yours!" Faby sang.

Samantha slipped into the bathroom. I lay back on the bed with a frustrated sigh and tried not to think about Samantha lathering her shapely limbs on the other side of that door.

Faby must have sensed the lingering tension in the air. "What'd I miss?"

"Nothing," I fibbed.

Faby pulled a brush through her wet hair. "If you want to kiss her, you should just kiss her already."

"It's that obvious, huh?"

"That you're head over heels in love? Yup."

"But she doesn't think of me that way," I said, hoping Faby would correct my assumption.

"She doesn't *not* think of you that way, either," Faby replied. "She's a tough nut to crack, we all know that. She's got that heart of hers encased in concrete so it won't get broken again. But you're already in there, D. She trusts you. The rest of it should be easy, especially with everything you've got goin' on."

"What about Tony?" I asked. Part of me still felt like a traitor for pursuing the love of my best friend's life.

Faby's face wrinkled up in disgust as if she'd just caught whiff of a foul smell. "What about him? You and I both know that Sam deserves better."

I'm not gonna lie, having Faby's blessing filled me with a renewed sense of purpose. In my heart, I'd never wavered about wanting to be with Samantha. I'd just been waiting. But waiting for what? Faby was right—you don't get the girl by sitting on the fence.

Chapter Seventeen

Samantha

After we all showered, the three of us headed out to explore the city. Our hotel was in a great location, just a few blocks from the River Seine and within walking distance of the majority of sights on Faby's must-see list.

I was surprised to learn that Damion actually knew a lot about France, even more than Faby. His area of expertise was class warfare, and he had spent a lot of time over the years studying the French Revolution, one of the most famous peasant uprisings in history. As we wandered through the city, he served as our tour guide, describing the significance of the various monuments we came upon.

"King Louis XVI and Marie Antoinette called this place home during the French Revolution," Damion explained as we explored the grounds and gardens of the *Tuileries Palace*. "When the peasants overthrew the monarchy, the king and queen lived here in pseudo-captivity for two years until their respective executions."

"I can think of worse places to spend my last days," Faby remarked. "A palace probably has way more amenities than your typical death row."

I've always had a soft spot for Marie Antoinette, who had been mischaracterized, misunderstood, and ultimately persecuted for daring to defy convention. Throughout history, too many women had lost their lives after being branded as whores or witches, put to death for alleged promiscuity and other moral offenses because men refused to let women step outside of the narrow, subservient roles society confined them to. The feminist in me stood in solidarity with all of them.

As we approached the *Place de la Concorde*, the square where Marie Antoinette and countless others lost their heads when death by guillotine was in vogue, my heart was heavy contemplating the centuries of injustice women had to endure, and *still* had to endure in some corners of the world. I was so glad to be born in America in the 20th century; I wouldn't have lasted long at all during one of the more oppressive eras.

We headed toward the *Champs Elysées* (the main drag in Paris) and found a cute little Parisian bistro with a reasonable prix fixe menu that allowed us to sample some of Paris's native cuisine. Damion was brave enough to order the *escargót*; served in a rich, buttery sauce, it was surprisingly tasty. My favorite part was dessert, *crème brûlée*, which was brought to the table *en enflammé*.

Over two bottles of French wine we enjoyed a lovely evening of food, conversation, and Parisian people-watching. For the first time since arriving in Europe, I actually felt like I was in a foreign country. The French were very proud of their culture, and unlike

Amsterdam, where English was common and spoken widely, the French did not go out of their way to accommodate foreigners. Since Faby was already fluent in Spanish, she studied French in high school and had a decent grasp of the language. She was able to put those years of instruction to good use as we wandered around Paris.

When we left the restaurant, stuffed and satiated from an excellent four-course meal, our gaze was immediately pulled toward the west where a shining tower of golden light stretched toward the heavens. I gasped, caught off guard by the brilliant beauty of the Eiffel Tower, gleaming in the night sky.

I've seen a lot of beautiful sights in my life, but the Eiffel Tower, all lit up like a Christmas tree in Rockefeller Center, truly took my breath away. Our excursion to the base could no longer wait until morning—we were drawn to the glowing structure like moths to a flame, making our way toward the light on foot.

I understood now why Paris was referred to as the "City of Lights." As we strolled along the riverbank, the soft glow from the street lamps reflected on the water, turning the river into a shimmering pool. The scenery was magical, the perfect setting for falling in love.

Just as that thought crossed my mind, Damion slipped his arm around my shoulder, drawing me to his side as we crossed the bridge, perfectly in step. He smelled amazing; he always did. Backlit by the glow from a street lamp, he looked so handsome staring down at me, his aura aflame, radiating warmth and compassion from his soft, brown eyes.

It was so confusing.

Guys like Damion don't exist in the real world. He reminded me of the heroes depicted in romance novels or soap operas—the ones who are just too good to be true. He always did the right thing and said the right thing. He's protective and accomplished, reliable and strong. The kind of guy you could bring home and your entire family—even your overprotective brothers—would be doing backflips.

You know that guy, right? He's the one who usually gets his heart broken by some unappreciative, undeserving girl.

See, that was the problem. Even if I could set aside the fact that I was hooking up with *Tony's best friend*, deep down I knew that I didn't deserve Damion. I was too damaged and jaded to receive the love he had to give, much less return it.

Faby called bullshit when I shared my theory with her.

"That is the most ridiculous thing I've ever heard," Faby argued. "Damion is a great guy and he is crazy about you. Why wouldn't you deserve someone bent on treating you like a queen? You're cockblocking your *damn* self with this nonsense about not being worthy—I don't get it."

"Geez, when did you become head cheerleader for Team Damion?"

"After I saw with my own eyes how perfect you are for each other."

I took a deep breath. "I don't think I'm capable of loving him back," I confessed. "Of loving anyone."

"Samantha Merrick, that might be the most depressing thing I have ever heard. You are 22 years old. You cannot let one bad experience—"

"Two," I corrected.

"—a *few* bad experiences turn you off love forever. That doesn't make any sense. A good man can heal your heart."

"That may be true, but Damion is not the right guinea pig for this experiment. If I take your advice and go for it, and you're wrong, my friendship with Damion will be ruined. It's not worth the risk."

"That's the fear talking," Faby countered. "Now set the fear aside for a moment and ask yourself this—what if I'm right?"

Chapter Eighteen

Damion

Man, this is some dreamy ish right here. The twinkling lights, the golden stream of the Seine, a glowing tower set against a starry sky. Hands down the most romantic place I'd ever been and I had the woman I love on my arm to boot. Everything about Paris amplified what I was already feeling—that I loved Samantha and wanted to spend my life with her. I'd reached complete and utter clarity on that point, just needed to make my move.

I almost kissed her on the bridge. We locked eyes and I could see that she, too, was lost in the magic. But she turned away before I could lean in.

I tried again at the base of the Eiffel Tower, as we shared yet another fleeting moment of intense connection. She didn't break away this time, but we were interrupted by a couple who wanted me to take their picture.

Maybe the Universe was trying to tell me something.

I'd been in London for almost a year, but this was only my second visit to Paris. In March, I had taken the ferry over by myself and wandered the streets in this strange land, lost and alienated because I didn't know a lick of French besides *Bonjour* and *Merci*. The French had an elitist air about them and were not particularly patient with clumsy, lost foreigners asking them questions in English. The anti-American sentiment I felt in London was even worse here, and as a result, I didn't enjoy myself very much. Which is why I hadn't been back. But this trip was a completely different experience. With my fearless road dawgs and Faby's ability to translate for us, I was seeing Paris in a whole, new light.

There were a lot of people out and about on this warm, July night. As we relaxed beside a fountain near the base of the tower, Faby struck up a conversation with a couple from Spain. They were en route to the Left Bank for cocktails and dancing.

"Join us," they insisted. "We can share a taxi to the club."

The couple, Felipe and Ana, were newlyweds in their late twenties. They had come to Paris, Ana's favorite city, for their honeymoon.

"How long have you two been together?" Ana asked Samantha, as Felipe and I tried to hail a cab.

Faby snickered. I watched Samantha with an amused look to see how she would respond.

The blush in Samantha's cheeks signaled her discomfort. "Me and Damion?" Samantha asked. "We're just friends."

"Why just friends?" Ana pressed. "He is so handsome and clearly in love with you."

"Thank you!" Faby exclaimed, giving Ana a high five. "I've been trying to tell her the exact same thing! She's the only one who doesn't see it."

Samantha ignored them both, creating a moment of awkward tension. Then a cab pulled up and we piled in—destination Left Bank.

Felipe and Ana took us to a trendy little club in Montparnasse with a rooftop bar that afforded gorgeous views of the city. We had a blast. After knocking back several rounds of drinks, we proceeded to tear it up on the dance floor as the DJ spun a mix of house music, hip hop, and American Top 40. The booze had done wonders for Samantha's mood, and she was teasing me to the brink of madness on the dance floor. When she wasn't grinding her backside against my groin, she had her arms wrapped tight around my neck as we moved to the beat. Then she'd spin away and grind up on Faby or some other random dude in the crowd, before eventually circling back to me. Elusive as ever, she never stayed close long enough for me to take hold. Like a fist full of water, she slipped through my fingers every time.

We returned to our hotel around 3 a.m. I glanced at the two twin beds; they weren't exactly suitable for sharing. Grabbing a blanket and pillow from the closet, I cleared a space on the floor near the window.

"What are you doing?" Faby asked.

"Making up my bed."

"Please, there is no need for you to sleep on that filthy floor," Faby replied. "You can share the bed with Sam…"

Chapter Nineteen

Samantha

Well, that sobered me right up.

I could have killed her. The last thing I needed was to share a bed with Damion.

"Uh, I'm not sure that's a good idea," I stammered.

"Why not?" Faby asked, blinking innocent eyes at me. "We're all family here. I'd offer to sleep with him but I know I'm going to be tossing and turning all night waiting for morning to get here. I'm just trying to help you out."

Sure you are, I thought. It was true though—I'd lived with Faby long enough to know that she was not exactly the most peaceful when at rest. Faby had vivid dreams that caused her to talk, and kick, in her sleep.

"I can sleep on the floor," Damion interjected. "I really don't mind."

"Don't be ridiculous," Faby said. "There's plenty of bed to go around."

I realized that continuing to protest was a waste of time and energy. With everyone and their grandma conspiring to get me into bed with Damion, resistance was futile. "Alright, fine," I said, climbing into the bed closest to the window. "I'm way too tired to argue."

Faby stood up with a satisfied smirk. "Great. Now that *that's* settled, I'm going down to the Business Center to get online. I need to put the finishing touches on tomorrow's itinerary. Don't wait up." She skipped out the door, letting it slam behind her.

Damion removed his shirt and changed into a white tank top, his muscular arms on display. Had he always been so buff? He had a phoenix, his power animal, tattooed on his left shoulder, and his brother's name in a band around his right bicep. I'd always been a fan of Damion's ink—tattoos were such a turn-on.

All of a sudden, the idea of cuddling up against his hard body didn't seem so bad.

"You sure you're cool?" he asked.

"Yeah, it's fine," I said, trying to pull my mind out of the gutter. "Faby's right—we're practically family."

"Ouch," Damion said, sliding into bed next to me. "That's even worse than being in the Friend Zone."

"Why? Because I expect you to be in my life forever, no matter what?"

"There are ways to have all that without casting me in the role of *brother*."

"Dame, you know I love you…"

"And here comes the 'But'," he said with a sigh. "There's always a 'But' in there somewhere."

Truth was, I didn't know what I was feeling anymore. My attraction to Damion was growing with each passing day, and my alcohol-fueled libido wasn't helping. Maybe Faby was right, maybe it would all be fine if I just got out of my own damn way.

"No buts," I whispered, settling into spooning position. I took his hand and wrapped his strong arm around my torso. "It's late. We have a long day tomorrow."

Without another word, Damion pulled me close, his warm breath on my neck and a sizeable erection pressed against my backside as we drifted off to sleep.

When Damion and I woke the next morning, Faby was nowhere to be found. There was a note on the nightstand:

Sorry, couldn't wait to explore the city. Meet me at the Castel Café, near the base of the Eiffel Tower, at 1 p.m.

"Like a kid on Christmas morning," I said, shaking my head. "Just couldn't wait to unwrap her present."

Damion stood up and stretched. I could see the outline of his six-pack underneath the thin cotton of his tank top. "You want the first shower?" he asked.

Yeah, a cold one.

I grabbed my towel. "Sure, I'll be quick."

When I emerged from the bathroom twenty minutes later, Damion had made a pot of coffee, croissants, and a bowl of fruit appear.

"Wow, this looks amazing," I said, taking a bite of the warm, flaky pastry.

"So do you," Damion said with a wink, before disappearing into the bathroom.

I smiled and sat down to enjoy my breakfast. His ability to anticipate and tend to my every need was indeed...magical. Who was I kidding—men like Damion were practically an endangered species.

There was one hurdle I couldn't quite get over though. For some reason, I just didn't feel an intense yearning for Damion the way I did with Tony. Tony had shown me what love was, and what we shared was my barometer. The incredible lows were only matched by the indescribable highs. A passion that burned hot and without reason. Damion, as wonderful as he was, just didn't make me *burn*...

I pondered that one for a minute. What is that about anyway? Why do intelligent women like myself frequently overlook the great guy standing right in front of us, relegating him to the Friend Zone, where he waits in the wings to console us when the bad boy of the moment breaks us into pieces? And he's always there to console us, EVERY TIME! Because the good guy is reliable like that, loyal like that. Yet we never give him a chance. Why does our heart make decisions so clearly and foolishly against our own self-interests?

The resultant epiphany was as striking as my first glimpse of the Eiffel Tower.

Maybe my love for Damion could grow. Like a soft ember, perhaps it just needed some nurturing, the right kindling, to burst into a righteous flame.

Chapter Twenty

Damion

Samantha and I spent the morning at the Eiffel Tower. While not as hypnotic as it had been at night, it was still an impressive structure. We took a glass elevator to the top and spent an hour up there enjoying views of the city in all directions.

Samantha snapped some pictures of the Arc de Triomphe in the distance. "I guess I can cross this off my bucket list."

"Bucket list, huh?" I took the camera as she posed for me. The smile on her face was genuine, and I was happy to document its return. "I didn't know you had a bucket list. What else you got on there?"

"Stuff."

"Oh yeah? What kinda stuff?"

She took the camera back and pointed it at me. "Well, a gondola ride in Venice is definitely on there, so that will make two items that I'm able to cross off during this trip. I also want to see the pyramids in Egypt and zipline in Costa Rica. Learn to surf. Experience Carnivál in Brazil, and Mardi Gras in New Orleans.

Attend the Cannes Film Festival. Oh, I really want to stay in one of those overwater bungalows in Bora Bora, too. You know, the ones that are out in the middle of the ocean."

"Those things are sick," I said, taking mental notes.

"I also want to design and build a cabin in the mountains somewhere, from the ground up. So I can have a sanctuary whenever I need to escape the city."

I loved that idea. Every nature lover should have a cabin in the woods for mental health purposes.

"What about you?" she asked. "What's on your 'must-do' list? Sky-diving? Running a marathon?"

"Actually, I haven't made an official bucket list."

"No time like the present," she said. "Come on, what are the wildest dreams you can conjure up?"

I gazed across the skyline. "Well, let's see. I plan to write several books, so it would be great to win a prestigious award for one of them. Then use the platform to start a nonprofit that serves underprivileged youth. Definitely want to take a trip to Africa. I'd also love to hike down into the Grand Canyon and converse with some Havasupai elders about their tribal customs and traditions. Maybe I could spend a few months down there with them, and then write a book about that. And of course with all these bestsellers, Oprah will want to have me on her show."

"Of course," she teased.

"But really, what I'm looking forward to most is having a wife and kids."

"You're going to be a great dad," Samantha said softly.

"Hopefully. If I'm lucky enough to find the right girl."

"You'll find her."

I turned her face toward mine. "What if I already have?"

As I stared into her eyes, Samantha did something I wasn't expecting—she leaned in.

That was all the invitation I needed. I didn't hesitate to close the distance between her lips and mine. She tasted like coconut chapstick. This wasn't our first kiss, but there was a passion present that wasn't there the first time and I drank it up. In fact, I don't think I've *ever* felt such a rush of lust, longing and... love.

I didn't want to let her go, in case the lowering of her defenses was some temporary lapse in judgment. The kiss was long and drawn out, one that might prompt an onlooker to shout "Get a room!" But seeing as how we were atop the Eiffel Tower, such a display wasn't necessarily out of place and we weren't chastised for our impromptu make-out session. Not that I would have cared—I'd waited too long for this moment.

Eventually, we came up for air. I caught my breath as her face came into focus. She was smiling up at me.

"Wow," was all I could think to say.

"Yeah, that was pretty much inevitable," Samantha said with a laugh.

"And long overdue."

"That, too."

We stared at each other for a long time, our eyes adjusting to this new picture. I'm not gonna lie—I liked what I saw.

"But how could this possibly work?" Samantha asked out of nowhere. "You live in London, and I—I don't know where the hell I'm going to be—"

"Stop it, don't do that," I interrupted.

"What?"

"Spin yourself in circles trying to figure out what's next. None of us can predict the future. Life unfolds; our job is to live it."

"But—"

"Always with the 'buts'." I halted her protest with another kiss. Turning her around, I gestured toward the Paris skyline. "Six months ago, did you think you'd be standing atop the Eiffel Tower, backpacking through Europe with your best friends?"

Samantha shook her head. "No, not in my wildest dreams."

"Yet, here you are. There's no way to know what life has in store for us, but there's also no reason to assume that it will be anything less than amazing. Yeah, maybe it will be hard, and maybe we'll get hurt. But this could also turn out to be the best thing that's ever happened to either one of us." I spun her back around. "There's only one way to find out."

She nodded. "Alright, I'm not going to fight anymore. I'm open to seeing where this goes."

I could *not* believe my ears.

"But I need to take things slow," she continued.

"We can go as slow as you want," I assured her, my heart racing with excitement.

"Good. You're my best friend, Dame. I don't ever want to lose that."

"Not possible. Friend or lover, I'm in this for the long haul. You can't lose me."

"Promise?"

"Promise."

And we sealed it with a kiss.

Faby immediately picked up on the change when she joined us for lunch.

"Well, well—what do we have here?" she asked, taking a seat beside Samantha.

Samantha was trying to decipher the menu, which was entirely in French. "Just trying to figure out what I want for lunch. What are *Les Crudités?*"

"Raw vegetables."

"Hmmm, that sounds boring. Can you order something for me?"

"How about an order of Damion with a side of happiness? Or is that what you had for breakfast?"

I laughed. "Jesus, nothing gets by you, does it?"

"Not really. I also got an eyeful of your PDA as I was crossing the river." Faby nudged Samantha with her elbow. "It's about damn time."

"We're taking things slow," Samantha insisted.

"Hey, I think the progression from stalled to slow is an excellent development. You guys knock those boots yet? Was it everything you imagined and more?"

I almost choked on my coffee when Faby let that one fly.

"Ha ha," Samantha said. She did not look amused. "Why don't you tell us how *your* day has been?"

In flawless French, Faby ordered a Perrier and a bowl of crab bisque for herself, a turkey sandwich for Sam, and a cheeseburger for me. "I'm having a blast," she said, after the waitress departed.

"I got a four-day Museum pass, which gives me free admission to most of the attractions *and* I get to bypass the lines. I've already been to Notre Dame and the Museum of Modern Art."

"Gosh, I feel like such an underachiever," Samantha said. "All we've done is visit the Eiffel Tower."

"That's not all. You've also surpassed a significant relationship milestone. I consider that quite an accomplishment."

Faby ain't ever lied. This was definitely the most eventful day of the trip thus far, the first of many, I hoped.

Chapter Twenty-One

Samantha

Paris was definitely a turning point in my relationship with Damion. As Damion waxed poetic about the uncertainty of life, challenging me to surrender to the flow, I found myself receptive to his pleas. He was right—we couldn't predict the future. Life had certainly taught me that. Maybe it would all be fine if I resisted the urge to self-sabotage by fixating on the least desirable outcome.

So I shut my mind off and let go...

What a lovely way to fall. With no fear of a painful or traumatic landing, I was able to immerse myself in the romance. A previous heartbreak can really impede your ability to give in when love comes knocking, making it hard to trust that when someone says they'll never leave, that they mean it. When you've been let down before, a part of you is always waiting for the other shoe to drop. But because my trust of Damion was total, I no longer feared the freefall into love's abyss. If there was one thing I could be sure of, it's that Damion would always be there to catch me.

Faby had a long list of sights to see in Paris, and since I had little interest in the art scene, we decided to split up and craft separate sightseeing excursions. It worked out perfectly—Faby was free to move through her to-do list at her preferred pace, and I was able to enjoy being with Damion. We'd meet up in the evening for dinner, then find a club or lounge where we could kick back and unwind.

On day three, at Faby's insistence, Damion and I decided to check out the Louvre, home to classic works of art like the Mona Lisa and Venus de Milo. Damion and I spent most of the day inside the massive museum, admiring the wall-size paintings, ceiling murals, and ancient statues. It was crazy how *old* some of this stuff was, each piece immortalizing the era in which it was created.

We migrated to the section of the Lourve that showcased Italian artists such as Michelangelo and Leonardo Da Vinci. I had an affinity for all things Italian, and enjoyed this section the most. I stared in awe at a piece painted in 1563. Titled, "The Wedding Feast at Cana," it depicted the feast where Jesus famously turned water into wine. There had to be over 100 figures on the wall-size canvas, members of the court in colorful attire, their facial expressions rendered in stunning detail.

I studied the image of Jesus, the centerpiece of the painting. "Do you think that's what Jesus really looked like?"

"Personally, I'm much more intrigued by the idea of a Black Jesus," he quipped.

"Of course you are," I said with a smile, as we strolled along hand in hand.

"Can you imagine the museums of the future?" Damion asked. "What artifacts do you think they'll use to represent the 80's and 90's?"

"You're assuming there are still museums," I replied. "At the rate we're going, funding for the Arts will be long gone by then."

"Such a pessimist." He kissed the top of my head. "We're going to have to do something about that."

"I'm not a pessimist, I'm a realist—there's a difference. But to answer your question, the ancient artifacts of our generation will probably consist of boomboxes, gold chains, and Backstreet Boys posters."

"And Hammer pants. Don't forget the Hammer pants."

We cracked up.

"Actually, the future's equivalent of the Louvre will probably be a Wax Museum the size of a small country, filled with replicas of athletes, celebrities and reality TV stars," Damion added.

I knew he was only half kidding. "Good lord, does our generation represent anything of substance?"

"I really don't think so." The smile faded from his face, replaced by a somber frown. "But it's not too late to change that."

I had no doubt in my mind that Damion would rise to that challenge one day. His determination to make a difference in this world was the driving force behind everything he did, and, like Faby, he was barreling down a path paved with promise. He knew exactly where he was going, which enabled him to put the bulk of his focus on getting there.

Oh, how I wished their clarity was contagious. Instead of moving toward a tangible goal, I was still backtracking, course correcting, and wandering in circles. I'm all for the road less traveled, but I wasn't even sure if I was on a road anymore.

"If there's a revolution to be had, I'm sure you'll be right at the center of it." I squeezed his hand. "And I'll be right there cheering you on."

"Mmmm, I like the sound of *all* that." He bent down for a kiss.

We kissed a lot, which was strange because PDA had never really been my style. I was used to dating guys who were much more private about their business. But Damion could not keep his hands or lips off me. Maybe it had something to do with the fact that we hadn't consummated our new relationship yet.

It's not that I didn't want to sleep with him. After our x-rated adventures in the Red Light District, I could definitely use a release. But I was scared to take it to the next level—for a bunch of reasons.

First of all, I was still learning to see Damion in a lustful way. Don't get me wrong, the man is *fine*. *Essence* 'Bachelor of the Month' material for sure. But I'd spent the past three years thinking of him as a brother figure. What if the sex was wack? Then what?

Thankfully, Damion didn't press the issue. I played it off like it felt awkward to be messing around while Faby was in the next bed, or that it was hard to relax when I knew she could walk in at any moment, and blah, blah, blah. The excuses were BS, and I'm pretty sure Damion knew it, but he didn't show an ounce of frustration or impatience. He seemed perfectly content holding me close every night and covering me with kisses every chance he got.

The slowed down courtship actually added to the romance. I hadn't taken this much time on the front end of a relationship since, well, Tony.

Ah, Tony. My other 'never to be spoken of' reason for delaying intimacy with Damion. Part of me was still trying to make peace with this betrayal, knowing that once Damion and I crossed that line, there would be no going back. For either of us.

Damion didn't speak on it, but I knew he missed Tony. And I could imagine, pride aside, that Tony missed Damion just as much. They had grown up together, boyhood friends, and I hated that I was the cause of their falling out. If I had one wish regarding the Tony situation, it would be to repair their fractured bond, an unintended casualty in our tragic love story.

However, after this latest turn of events, a reconciliation between Tony and Damion was looking less and less likely.

Chapter Twenty-Two

Damion

When Faby met up with us for dinner that night, she had a guy with her.

"Hi," she said, giving us each a kiss on each cheek. She'd been doing that for the past two days whenever we said hello or goodbye. "This is Jean Paul. Jean Paul, these are my friends Samantha and Damion."

Since I'd come to view Faby as a sister, my protective instinct was instantly activated. I shook Jean Paul's hand, sizing him up. He was a clean-cut European with sandy brown hair and a Brad Pitt look that could flip from good guy to bad boy with the arch of an eyebrow. When he greeted us, a thick, French accent coated his words.

We got to know Jean Paul over dinner. Any reservations I had slowly dissipated as the evening wore on. Jean Paul was Swiss, an IT consultant by profession, but also a recent graduate of the prestigious Sorbonne in Paris with a degree in French and Comparative Literature. He was volunteering at the Musée d'Orsay for the summer, until his next consulting gig started in September.

"Balance is very important to me," he said in perfect English, "and it is very easy to become isolated when you work with technology and machines. The money is good, but there is a trade-off. That's why I volunteer at the museum, to make sure that I spend equal amounts of time surrounded by beauty." His eyes lingered on Faby's face.

Faby was hanging on his every word. "That's where we met," she explained. "He noticed me studying the museum map, asked if I needed help, and next thing I knew he was taking me on a personalized tour. Can you believe his next assignment is to build a design interface at one of Paris's leading architecture firms? How's *that* for a coincidence, huh Dame?"

I smiled at her. "Sounds like y'all have a lot in common."

"Tell them what else you're working on," Faby prodded.

Jean Paul sat up a little straighter and cleared his throat. "I'm good with computers—it comes naturally for me, understanding code and programming—but my real passion is writing. I consider IT my side job. I can live off a two-week assignment for several months if I live simply, which I do because that is how I was raised. I use the down time in between jobs to focus on my book."

Intrigued, I asked, "What is your book about?"

"My novel is set in post-apocalyptic France after World War III. Most of continental Europe has been decimated, and the task of rebuilding has fallen to a group of French gypsies and mystics, who correctly prophesized the fall of modern civilization. They have been elevated, quite unwillingly, to the status of gods by the survivors of the war. This new generation of leaders revisit the theories and texts that emerged during the Enlightenment period for guidance on the path forward. With those theories as their foundation, they strive to erect an alternative society, one that encourages spiritual, as well as material, pursuits."

And with that, Jean Paul had officially won me over.

Faby had clearly been won over as well. In addition to being an art lover, Jean Paul was intelligent, well-traveled, and fluent in *four* languages. A true renaissance man.

I needed to step my game way up.

After dinner, JP invited us back to his place to hang out. Charles, his roommate, was another well-mannered, highly educated fellow with grand aspirations. I liked him, too. Over several bottles of French wine and some damn good hash, we exchanged ideas and impressions about our respective cultures. Like Faby, I'm a classic extrovert; I enjoy meeting new people and picking their brains about various things. Conversation and debate were my life blood, and my present company was top notch on both counts.

Coincidentally, Charles grew up in a white, working class community in Northern England and had his own distinct perspective on the class warfare that led to the race riots of 2001, one of the events I was researching for my book. My research had been on the back burner since Samantha and Faby showed up on my doorstep, but talking to Charles about my work reinvigorated me. I felt compelled to mine him for data, and Charles was open, articulate, and sans prejudice. He answered each of my questions with thoughtful insight.

It was four in the morning when we decided to call it a night.

"You guys are more than welcome to stay over," JP said as he cleared the empty bottles and glasses from the coffee table. "The futon is quite comfortable."

"I appreciate the offer," I said, "but I think we're gonna grab a cab back to the hotel. You coming, Fab?"

Faby's lustful gaze was fixed on our host. "No, I think I'm going to stay here. JP promised to take me to Versailles in the morning."

"You should come with us," JP insisted. "We can pick you up on the way. Do you think you could be ready by noon?"

I glanced at Samantha. She was not exactly a morning person.

Samantha nodded. "Sounds like a plan. Thanks again for everything, JP—this has been a great night."

JP called us a cab and we waited on the curb for it to arrive. I held Samantha close, anxious to get back to the hotel. Now that we finally had the room to ourselves, I was hoping tonight would be the night. I'd been doing my best to be patient about the no-sex situation, but I was still a man. It was damn hard to lay next to the woman you love and just cuddle. But with Faby at JP's, there was nothing preventing us from taking things to the next level. I'd have plenty of time to show Samantha how I really felt, that there *was* chemistry there, that I was just as good a man as Tony.

Men are competitive by nature, so of course I felt like I had something to prove. The memory of Tony was all up in this relationship, and I was very conscious of the fact that not only did I have to win her heart, I had to make her forget about Tony… no small feat seeing as how they were "soulmates." And I don't mean that in some sarcastic, flippant way, either. They *were* soulmates. I was there, I witnessed their love with my own eyes. But I also believed you could have more than one soulmate in any given lifetime. All I needed was for Samantha to believe it, too.

Chapter Twenty-Three

Samantha

Well, I'm happy to report that my fears that Damion and I might lack sexual chemistry were completely unnecessary.

With all the sexual tension that had built up over the years, I figured when we finally did the deed, it would be fast and furious. Clothes being ripped off and flung about the room, hungry mouths gasping and biting with urgency. But our first time didn't resemble a hastily choreographed dance at all; it was a smooth and graceful Viennese waltz.

He started with a full body massage. After all the walking we'd been doing, this was a real treat. He took his time massaging my feet, calves and thighs before moving up to my butt (which I'm sure he enjoyed as much as I did). His strong hands eased the knots out of my sore muscles as I melted into the bed. When he reached my neck, he flipped me over and worked his way back down my body, this time using his mouth as his guide. His tongue traced the curves of my breasts and the dip in my belly button before he settled in to feast between my legs.

I have to say, I was pretty impressed with his skills. Damion was as patient, tender, and attentive in his lovemaking as he was with everything else. He took his time, savoring every touch, every taste. I came twice for every orgasm Damion had, a ratio he insisted on. I certainly wasn't complaining—I'd had enough bad sex to know how rare this was. We made love until the sun came up, enjoying a level of sexual compatibility I hadn't experienced since...

Yep, you guessed it. Tony.

I know it's shitty to compare the two. Crude, even. But I couldn't help it. Tony was my barometer for what love was supposed to look and feel like. What passion was supposed to look and feel like. Damion had to at least match, if not exceed, my feelings for Tony. Our survival as a couple depended on it.

Unfortunately, as great as the sex was, it was not nearly as intense as what I shared with Tony. Tony and I made love like our lives depended on it, fully in the moment, with a breathless, all-consuming urgency. Sex with Damion, in contrast, was all about sensuality, savoring our feast instead of scarfing it down. Being with Damion felt warm and safe, while being with Tony felt like I was on fire.

"I don't think one type of passion is necessarily better than the other," Faby offered. We had just arrived at the Palace of Versailles and had stopped for a bathroom break while the boys stood in line for coffee at the café. "We need different things at different times."

"And did you get what you *needed* last night?" I asked, though the question was purely rhetorical. I could tell from the smile on her face that things with JP had gone really, really well. She was glowing. I wondered if I was sporting a similar shine.

Faby gave a wistful sigh. "JP is amazing. In every way. Simply amazing."

I had to agree. Jean Paul, like Damion, was one of those too-good-to-be-true, total package type of guys. A *man*, with intellect, ambition, and life experiences. Something to offer, something to say. We were all enjoying his company.

"Any chance you can talk him into coming with us when we head down to Switzerland?" We were eleven days into our trip and needed to keep it moving if we wanted to have time left for Italy. Our flight back to the States departed from Rome on August 2nd.

"Not only is he down to travel with us, but he already called ahead to his folks. They have enough room for us all to stay for a few days. Free of charge."

"Are you serious?" I could not get over the ease with which things just fell into place over here. This was the longest streak of good luck I'd ever had.

"Yup. If it's cool with you and Damion that JP joins us."

"I can't imagine Damion having a problem with it."

Faby linked her arm with mine as we floated back to our men. "Can you believe this?"

"No," I said. "I really can't."

The Palace of Versailles was also pretty unbelievable. Home to generations of French royalty, the palace was an enduring testament to excess and opulence. The rooms were huge, some with vivid murals covering the walls and ceilings, each a mini-masterpiece. The grounds were just as impressive, with expansive lawns, immaculate landscaping, and fountains adorned with Roman gods situated throughout the property. I'd never seen anything like it.

The massive estate spanned over two thousand acres. Toward the northeastern part of the property, Marie Antoinette had created a rustic retreat where she could escape the formality of palace life. Several storybook structures dotted the edge of a tranquil lake, complete with a water wheel, small tower, and a farm that was home to a variety of animals. Though the grounds were littered with tourists snapping photos and gazing with wide eyes at their surroundings, there was a stillness and serenity about the place. I could see why the young queen loved it here.

"Now this is more like it," I said, taking a breath of fresh air. "I would much rather live out here in the country than in that big, lonely palace."

"Not feelin' the Hall of Mirrors, huh?" Damion asked.

"Don't get me wrong—Versailles' beauty is undeniable. But with so many people living in poverty, how can you justify living in such excess? Even if I was able to afford a huge mansion, I'd rather raise my kids in modest accommodations. Instill them with some down-to-earth values."

Damion held my hand as we headed toward the main house. "How big is this family you dream of? All the walks and talks we've had over the years, and you've never mentioned kids."

Damion was right—having children was one topic I never spoke on because I still carried around significant wounds surrounding my miscarriage. The thought of being pregnant again filled me with fear and anxiety, and my instinct was to avoid things that made me anxious.

"Of course I want to have kids," I said quickly. "Someday."

"How many?" he pressed.

I hesitated. This was no longer casual chitchat amongst friends; these were grown-up relationship questions.

The way you assess a long-term partner is different than the way you approach an affair. You can relax your standards when you're having a fling because you know it's temporary. But when you're talking about spending *the rest of your life* with someone, it was critical to be on the same page about the important stuff. A disconnect on something like having kids could be a deal-breaker, and it was best to unearth those incompatibilities early in a relationship.

"I don't know," I replied, that anxious feeling taking root in the pit of my stomach. "Not really attached to a particular number as long as they're healthy. What about you?"

"I've always wanted a huge family," he said with a big smile. "Four sons would be awesome. And a couple of daughters."

My heart skidded to a stop. "Six kids?"

Damion tried to maintain a straight face, but collapsed in laughter. "Naw, I'm just playing with you."

I punched him in the arm. "*Not* funny."

"I beg to differ. That look of horror on your face was priceless."

"That's a lot of damn kids!"

He wrapped me up in one of his all-encompassing hugs. "I'd be happy with two kids or twelve, as long as they all look like you."

I buried my head in his chest so he couldn't see how freaked out I was. The last time I dared to dream of being a wife and mother, I ended up with my heart broken into a hundred pieces. Life had taught me that it was dangerous to buy into that fantasy. Yet here was this man, asking me to believe, making the impossible seem possible.

I wanted to believe him. I really did. I'd come a long way in the thawing of my heart, but I wasn't sure if I was ready to surrender to the hope of happily ever after. Not yet anyway.

Chapter Twenty-Four

Damion

When Faby was ready to leave Paris, the four of us rode the rails down to Switzerland. It was great having another guy around. Not only did he add some much needed male energy to the mix, his presence liberated Sam and I from any guilt we felt about being coupled up. With JP rounding out the group, Faby was no longer a third wheel. The trip devolved into a free-for-all of hand-holding, stolen kisses, and all manner of mushiness.

Since we were on his home turf, JP took over tour guide duties, providing us with a locals introduction to Switzerland. Bordered to the north by France, the east by Germany and Austria, and the south by Italy, Switzerland was an intersection of cultures, a multilingual and multicultural population melting in a pot of peaceful coexistence. Known for its pristine beauty (littering will net you a hefty fine), efficiency (the sophisticated Swiss rail system was *always* on time), and independence (they maintain their own currency, the Swiss Franc, and refuse to join the European Union), the Swiss indeed marched to the beat of their own drum.

I was intrigued by the history of this tiny country— considering its proximity to battle, Switzerland's ability to stay out of both World Wars was impressive.

We disembarked in Lausanne, a town in the "French" part of Switzerland, and took the metro down to the lakefront district. After picking up sandwiches and snacks at the grocery store, we settled down for a picnic.

"This is one of my favorite cities on Lake Geneva," JP explained. "My sister is a professor at the University of Lausanne, and my oldest brother also went to school there. Lausanne is like a second home to me."

JP was the youngest of six siblings—four boys and two girls. His parents owned a hostel on Lake Brienz, a family business that went back several generations on his father's side. Claire, JP's mother, was the daughter of a French winemaker and schoolteacher. She had been raised and educated in the finest French schools, and met JP's father while skiing in the Swiss Alps with her college classmates. It had been love at first sight, and the two were married six months after Claire graduated from the Sorbonne. Claire gladly left the glitz and glamour of cosmopolitan Paris behind to settle into a simple life in the country, raising her kids and helping her husband run the hostel.

"My mother chose country life over the city, but it was always important to her that we had the privilege of having that same choice for ourselves. She insisted that we all go to college. My two oldest brothers graduated and returned to Brienz; they will most likely take over the family business one day. My third brother is currently traveling the world with friends—the last postcard we received was from Thailand. My oldest sister is a finance attorney in Zurich, and my sister Elise, who you'll meet tonight, is a professor of Psychology."

The richness of a large family was something I envied. JP had true roots—a place he could always return to. I wasn't sure such a place existed for me, but I was anxious to create it.

"Where do you think you'll end up?" I asked JP. "Do you ache for travel, or would you prefer to settle down in your native country?"

"I would like to do some traveling," he said, "but Switzerland is my home. Of course I'm biased, but I find this to be the most wonderful country in the world. When I leave Paris, I will probably settle down here in Lausanne."

I could see why Lausanne appealed to him. The town maintained its old world charm, but had the diversity and youthful energy of a college town—the best of both worlds. Where would Samantha and I end up? And would we be together? JP was giving me lots of food for thought.

JP's sister, Elise, met us at the Farmer's Market in Lausanne. She was a slender woman in her early-forties with long, silver-streaked hair. Exuding warmth and hospitality, she embraced us like we were kin. This must be a Frisch family trait—I'd never met people so welcoming. As a black man, this wasn't the response I typically elicited from strangers.

When we were done shopping, we loaded our bags into her Saab and headed up to the four-bedroom villa she shared with her partner, Christian. Elise and Christian were both professors at the

University. Though they weren't married, they'd been together for seventeen years, living in the foothills of the Swiss Alps with their two dogs and three cats in non-wedded bliss.

"Elise is actually the one opposed to marriage," Christian explained as we relaxed on the patio. "She wants to make sure she is free to flee if something better comes along."

"I heard that!" Elise yelled from the kitchen. She and Faby were turning the fresh produce we'd acquired at the Farmer's Market into dinner.

"In all seriousness, we feel the strength of our commitment is more powerful being un-wed," Christian explained. Elise emerged from the kitchen with a tray of cheeses and warm bread and took a seat on his lap. "We are not staying together because we *have* to—we are staying together because we *want* to."

"I love your approach to commitment," Samantha said. She clinked glasses with Christian. "Love should not require a label to be considered valid."

"I don't know," Faby interjected, joining us. "For me, it's about more than a label. There is something sacred about taking vows in the church, before God and your loved ones. I understand that many people turn weddings into a circus, but the sentiment and ritual of uniting two lives and families is something to be celebrated. I respect where you're coming from, but personally, I very much look forward to getting married."

"Indeed, she's been planning the blessed event since she was seven," Samantha teased. "And I would put money on the fact that *your* wedding is going to fall more on the circus side of the continuum."

"Whatever. People love parties and I love throwing them." Faby stuck out her tongue.

"Well, call me old-fashioned," I added, "but I'm a marriage guy, too. I'll pass on the big, fancy wedding unless my girl wants one ..." I winked at Sam. "But I do look forward to being a husband. Very much."

"Well, who knew Americans were so romantic," Christian joked. He raised his glass. "To love!"

Thanks to our generous hosts, we were treated to another great night of stimulating conversation with new friends over good food and fantastic local wine. It was the perfect pit stop, not just because Elise and Christian were awesome company, but because the free food and lodging were giving my wallet a break. We'd been on the road for almost two weeks, and funds were starting to run low. The last thing I wanted to do was leave Samantha and Faby and head back to London, but I wasn't sure how much longer I could hang. I didn't believe in credit cards (another form of slavery), so when the money ran out, I'd have to head home.

There was also the issue of my book. I was in London on a funded fellowship, and the expectation was that I would have a publishable manuscript by the end of my stay. I hadn't written anything in weeks, and was dreading the next meeting with my advisor. As much fun as we were having, reality was starting to intrude, reminding me that at some point, the endless summer would indeed have to end. No amount of denial was going to change that fact.

Chapter Twenty-Five

Samantha

The next morning, Christian and Elise sent us off on the next leg of our journey with warm wishes and full bellies. We continued on to Lake Brienz, in the heart of Switzerland, to spend a few days at the Frisch family hostel.

I've never enjoyed a train ride so much. We were on the "Golden Pass" route, one of the scenic trains that traversed Switzerland, and every moment during our two and a half hour trip was a feast for the eyes. As the train wound its way into the heavily forested Alps, we left all evidence of the city behind. Quaint farmhouses dotted the rural landscape, the throngs of finely-dressed Parisians and café-littered boulevards replaced by rolling hillsides and... livestock. This storybook land of charming mountain towns was the antithesis of the glittering Parisian metropolis in every way, only hours away, yet worlds apart.

Mother Nature had really outdone herself. Cows and goats grazed lazily on the lush, green carpet of grass that covered the verdant pastures. Brilliant blue lakes reflected snow-capped mountain peaks in their tranquil waters, amplifying the beauty. I didn't think it could get any more beautiful, and then I caught a glimpse of the turquoise waters of Lake Brienz. I had never seen that color in nature before in my life.

Breathtaking at every turn, Switzerland was *this close* to dethroning Amsterdam as my favorite European locale. I was falling in love with every serene, unspoiled, immaculate inch.

To our delight, the hostel was located right on the banks of Lake Brienz. The three-story, twelve-room chalet had all the comforts of home—a great room filled with plush sofas surrounding a large, stone fireplace; a dining room with long, wooden tables for group meals; a game room complete with board games and a pool table; and two floors of dorm rooms that could accommodate between two and twenty occupants. JP's mother cooked dinner for all the guests each night, and everyone sat down to eat together, family-style, at 8 p.m.

Down by the lake, there was a sandy beach for sunbathing, and an assortment of innertubes, canoes, and kayaks you could rent if you wanted to spend the day on the water. With every comfort of home and all these fantastic amenities, we were more than pleased with our accommodations. That we'd stumbled upon all of this, free of charge, was icing on the cake.

JP's parents and brothers, like his sister, were warm and welcoming, rolling out the red carpet in anticipation of our arrival. JP hadn't been home in four months, and his mother was so excited about his visit. She couldn't stop hugging and kissing him, much to his embarrassment.

"Mama, *ça suffit!*"

"Pfft, if you came home more often, I wouldn't have to miss you so much."

We spent four lovely days at the hostel, which served as home base for our Swiss excursions. There was so much to see and do, and JP made sure we experienced the best of what the region had to offer. We lounged by the lake, but also rode cable cars and funiculars that whisked us to the mountain peaks surrounding Interlaken. There was something divine about hiking at extreme elevations. High above the mundane matters of the world, you truly feel closer to heaven. Or maybe that was an altitude-induced delusion. Either way, frolicking amongst the clouds was a surreal experience.

We also traveled to the town of Leukerbad, which was known for its natural hot springs. This was definitely a highlight of the trip for me, as soaking my body in hot water is one of my favorite pastimes. We spent the entire afternoon enjoying the mineral baths at Burgerbad, a huge, three-story facility with a number of pools at varying temperatures where locals and tourists could soak their troubles away. They even had a few waterslides on the property, and we giddily engaged our inner 10-year-olds as we sped down the slides in innertubes.

It was the most fun I'd had in a long time.

"An interesting piece of trivia I think you'll appreciate," JP began. We were soaking in Burgerbad's Turkish bath, a dark, steamy cave filled with the hottest water on the property. "The American writer, James Baldwin, loved to visit Leukerbad for leisure and retreat. He wrote *Guest in a Small Village* here."

"No way," Damion exclaimed. "Very cool."

If I were a writer, I would totally seek out places, just like this, for inspiration. I appreciated the relaxed pace, the stillness, the quiet time alone with my thoughts. Far away from the distractions of the modern world, each day we spent in the Alps brought me increased clarity. My heart's desires were slowly coming into focus.

I hadn't quite honed in on an exact course, but I had gotten very clear about what I *didn't* want. As I watched JP's parents, not just content, but undeniably fulfilled in their blissful simplicity, I realized I had no desire to keep up with the Joneses. I was not going to waste away in a soulless job that I hated, just so I could pay my bills. Money and the pursuit of *things* were not going to drive my decision-making process, and if I had to live off the grid to protect this mindset, so be it.

After spending our last day in Switzerland visiting Lucerne, we decided to split up. It was July 26th, and we were scheduled to fly back to the States from Rome in just six days. I couldn't believe we'd been abroad for almost three weeks—time really did fly when you were having fun. Damion had a friend in Munich that he wanted to visit (another opportunity for free lodging), and Faby wanted to check out the French Riviera. Knowing we were leaving Faby in JP's very capable hands, we agreed to part ways and meet back up in Venice, Italy in three days.

I couldn't believe we were nearing the end of the trip. A light cloud had descended on all of us as the fate of our blossoming relationships hung in the balance. We'd found something so rare and special in our respective companions; that it would all be forced to end in a matter of days was the harshest of reality checks.

Chapter Twenty-Six

Damion

My buddy Craig lived in Munich. We met in college while we were both at the University of Oregon. After graduation, I headed to UCSC for grad school, while Craig joined the Peace Corps to teach Math and Science in Kenya. While in Africa, he met a civic-minded German girl who was volunteering in a neighboring town and fell in love. He followed her back to Germany and married her. Ole Craig now called Munich home.

I used to give him shit for being so whipped that he felt compelled to relocate to another damn country. Back then, I thought that kind of move, *for a woman,* was sheer foolishness. Don't get me wrong—I *love* women. But they are fickle creatures. The old me never would have cosigned on a buddy uprooting his entire life for some chick. Not in a million years.

I was singing a completely new tune now, though. My sprung ass would do anything to avoid being separated from Samantha.

After waiting so long for her to come around, I wasn't trying to go back to the Friend Zone. That was not an option.

Samantha and I hadn't talked at all about how we were going to maintain this relationship long distance. Assuming she intended to maintain it. Maybe this whirlwind love affair fell into the "fling" category for her. She seemed serious, but she was, at the end of the day, a woman.

Fickle.

Actually, fickle was not the right adjective to describe Samantha. No, that word would be *torn*. She had a brilliant, analytical mind, but her penchant for analysis was as much a curse as a blessing. Samantha was forever second-guessing herself, keeping intimate relation with the past and regarding the future with ample skepticism. She had a lot on her mind already as she tried to figure out her next steps—the last thing I wanted to do was give her something else to agonize over.

I wasn't someone who normally shied away from tough talks. I was very pro-communication, a fan of the direct approach. But for some reason, I was all too happy to avoid the subject of Samantha's departure and our uncertain future. Even as the clock ticked down, denial held onto its appeal. Why wake from the dream prematurely?

Our mutual avoidance came to a screeching halt that evening. We were at the famous *Hofbrauhaus*, one of Germany's largest beer gardens, with Craig and his wife, Uschi. Enormous mugs filled with frothy ales and lagers sat in front of us as Germans and tourists from all corners of the globe shared life stories and anecdotes at long, wooden tables. We were only a few sips into our first round when Uschi broached the dreaded subject.

"When are you heading back to the States?" she asked Samantha.

Samantha's lips formed a soft pout. "My friend and I are flying home on Tuesday."

"Oh, wow—that's soon," Uschi said. I think she realized (a little too late) that she'd steered us onto a sensitive topic.

"Too soon," Samantha agreed. Her eyes welled up and she blinked back tears.

Uschi leaned forward, her eyes filled with empathy and concern. "I know exactly what you're going through. When I left Craig behind in Kenya to return to Germany, I felt like my heart was being ripped out. There is nothing harder than being apart from the one you love."

Samantha nodded, then stood and excused herself.

"Oh no, did I say something wrong?" Uschi asked.

"I think it's finally starting to sink in that she has to leave," I said. "Neither one of us is ready for this trip to be over."

"How much longer are you planning to stay in London?" Craig asked.

"I've got another year on this fellowship, but I also have a couple of job prospects if I want to extend my stay."

"And Samantha? What's her plan?"

I took a swig of my beer. "She's still figuring things out."

"So you're gonna do the long distance thing, huh?"

"I guess."

Uschi went to check on Samantha while Craig ordered another round. "You're really into this girl, aren't you?" he asked.

I flashed back through me and Samantha's complicated past—the ups, downs, and delays. "I've waited a long time for her," I said. "She's the One. She's always been the One."

"Well, in that case," Craig said, "let me put in a plug for love. Everyone thought I was crazy to stay out here for some woman."

"I know," I said with a chuckle. "I was one of them."

"Right. But I can tell you this, my friend—I have never regretted my decision to move to Germany. Not once. I gave up a lot to live as an ex pat half a world away from everything I know. But as corny as it sounds, home for me is where Uschi is. That woman is my world. I'd be happy in a windowless shack in Antartica, as long as she was by my side."

Once again, the old me would have given him all kinds of grief for taking such a soft position. Relationships come and go, and I used to believe it was risky to alter one's course for someone whose path may or may not be heading in the same direction as yours. But all that cynicism existed before I knew what it felt like to be in love, really in love. Before I'd experienced firsthand the highs that compelled lovers to do crazy, reckless things. Love made you feel like anything was possible. Thanks to Samantha, I'd become a believer, and I was ready to go all in.

Chapter Twenty-Seven

Samantha

Making the transition from Switzerland to Germany was a bit jarring. We were back in the hustle and bustle of civilization, with cars and traffic and crowded squares. Everything was super-sized here—from beer mugs to food portions to the decibel of people's voices in conversation. I had to fight off major claustrophobia while we were at the *Hofbrauhaus*; after adjusting to the slowed down pace of life in Switzerland, my senses just weren't ready for all that noise.

I was really grateful when Craig suggested we take his car and drive out to Bavaria for the day. Bavaria, a land of storybook villages and medieval fortresses, was located about an hour outside of Munich in the German countryside. It felt great to be in the country again, speeding along the highway with the windows down, the sweet taste of freedom on the breeze.

We did a drive-by of Crazy Ludwig's castle, perched precariously on a forested mountaintop. I'd seen castles like this depicted in fairy tales, but had no idea such structures actually existed in the real world.

"Jesus, I feel like I'm in a Disney movie," I said. A thin layer of fog tickled at the treetops, simultaneously romantic and somewhat menacing.

Damion pulled over so I could take some pictures. "That was actually the inspiration for Malificent's castle in Sleeping Beauty," he said.

"For real? I can totally see that. Wow."

The surrounding towns also had that old world, Disney charm. As I strolled along the cobblestone streets, I felt as if I'd stepped into a period piece. But I loved it. I was much more at ease in a small town than in the congested epicenter of the city. That's probably why I ended up at UC Santa Cruz (which is literally located in the middle of a forest) over nearby UCLA or the prestigious UC Berkeley. I was definitely a country girl at heart; the past week had certainly affirmed that.

Four more days. I couldn't believe I had to leave this magical place and return "home." If only I was returning to somewhere cool like the Bay Area, or Santa Cruz even. After this excellent adventure, how was I supposed to go back to the smoggy, materialistic, image- and status-obsessed culture that prevailed in Los Angeles? Back to living with my *mother*. God, I was not ready for *any* of that.

My intuition was sounding the alarms, and deep down I knew that LA was the wrong move for me. And while it was nice to finally have some clarity about something, the realization only made me more upset about my imminent departure.

"You should stay here in Europe with me," Damion said, as I vocalized my anxieties over lunch. We had picked up sandwiches and were picnicking in one of the town's many squares.

I straightened up, stunned. "What?"

"Well, seeing as how you're still in limbo, what is the difference between being in limbo in California or being in limbo over here?"

I couldn't believe what he was suggesting. "Damion, that's crazy. I don't have a job. I don't think I can even get a job out here. I have no way to support myself."

"But you have me. My fellowship pays pretty well. Housing is covered and I have enough cushion every month to cover groceries for an extra person. And I'm sure you could get a work visa and find part-time work somewhere, if you wanted to."

Damion had clearly given the proposal some thought. "You're serious, aren't you?"

"I know we haven't talked about the future and where this is going, and maybe I'm being presumptuous, but we've got a good thing here. I love you. I have every intention of spending the rest of my life with you. I don't want you to leave. I would do anything to have you by my side. It's where you belong."

Damn, he was not playing around.

"Look, this doesn't have to be a permanent thing—you can stay six more weeks or six more months. But why rush home when there's nothing to rush home for?"

It all made so much sense when he put it like that. Wow. My head was spinning as I tried to process such a drastic change of plans.

"It's such a generous offer, babe." I began. "I don't know what to say…"

"Say yes."

Chapter Twenty-Eight

Samantha

"You're going to stay here?" Faby asked in disbelief. "For how long?"

We had reunited in Venice, as planned, and were enjoying some of Italy's signature gelato as we strolled along the Grand Canal. The boys walked ahead of us; we had fallen behind to partake in a little girl talk.

"I don't know," I replied. "It's not like I have a reason to rush back."

"Wow."

"Wow? That's it? No, 'you're crazy' or 'how irresponsible?' "

"Come on, the last thing I'm trying to do is hate on love. If I didn't have that internship waiting for me, I'd probably do the same thing. I'd love to have more time with Jean Paul."

I could tell from the look on Faby's face that the thought of leaving Jean Paul was tearing her up inside. I don't think either of them expected to actually fall in love out here.

Shoot, that made three of us.

"Have you guys talked about what's next?" I asked softly.

Faby shook her head. "There's no need—we set the ground rules up front. Knowing this thing had an expiration date, we committed to having a wild and crazy, in-the-moment, no-holds-barred, love affair. And we succeeded—the past few weeks have been the stuff of legends. Have I developed feelings for him? Of course, he's awesome. Am I going to miss him? Absolutely. But my path is bringing me back to LA. This adventure has to end for the next one to begin."

"Well, that's a very grown up way of looking at the situation. I wonder if it's too late for Damion and I to strike a similar agreement."

"Your situation is totally different. You guys are not a fling; there's something real there that you should be building on." She paused. "I'm proud of you for sticking this out instead of running away."

No one can call you out on your shit like your best friend, right? The fact that my "flight" response hadn't been triggered was indeed out of character. I'd completely abandoned my self-protective code of non-attachment. Maybe it had to do with the fact that Damion and I started off with a solid friendship and were already very much attached. I never felt the need to run from him. As a matter of fact, my instinct was usually to run *towards* him. It's easy to fall for your best friend because so much of what binds a couple (compatibility, trust, common interests) is already there. But despite all the obvious reasons why this should work, I still felt pretty confused about things. Was Damion really the

139

One? I honestly didn't know. As magical as the past few weeks had been, threads of doubt lingered. I hadn't experienced this kind of emotional uncertainty with Tony; in fact, it had been the opposite. With Tony, I'd spent most of my time trying to talk myself *out* of feeling what I was feeling, cursing the bond we had when a future between us was no longer a possibility. Even now, there was still a part of me that belonged to Tony, a quiet yearning banished deep into the recesses of my fragile heart.

There was no denying that Damion was a wonderful man, worthy of my love, trust, and devotion. He would never leave me or hurt me the way Tony had. What I felt for Damion was strong, it was just *different*. And still relatively new. Maybe it would continue to brighten and deepen as time went on, and eventually grow to rival what I shared with Tony.

Only time would tell.

Italy was a wondrous land, with feasts for the eyes, ears, and taste buds in ample supply. But to experience Italy while you were in love was a whole other experience. The four of us had a blast exploring Venice, one of the most romantic cities in the world.

Like Amsterdam, Venice was built around a system of canals, a floating metropolis. Barred to automobile traffic, tourists and residents made their way around town on foot or via boat. It was amazing how much the absence of cars altered the vibe of a city. Once again, the pace of life slowed way down. We wandered through the narrow *calli* all day, allowing ourselves to get lost in the maze of cobblestone lanes and bridges, taking in the sights, sounds, and smells of this magnificent country.

I loved everything about Italy.

I loved the sensual language that was so pleasing to my ears. I could listen to people speak Italian all day. Though I often failed to understand what people were asking me, for some reason my response was always *yes*…

I loved the way strangers greeted us with a heartfelt and enthusiastic *"Buongiorno!"* when we passed them on the street.

I loved that you could find gelato on almost every block, and that the creamy delicacy came in endless flavors.

I loved the pizza, with thin, crispy crusts that served as a bed for perfectly paired toppings and cheesy goodness.

I loved the leisurely way Italians approached the act of dining. Meals stretched over hours with several, delectable courses. I couldn't help but compare the practice to the fast food culture that had colonized America. I'd had many excellent and substantial meals at places like the Cheesecake Factory, but I couldn't recall ever savoring and *tasting* food like I was doing here.

I loved that Italians valued "down time" enough to institute a widely adhered to "siesta" where shops and services closed for several hours each afternoon. Entire neighborhoods took one coordinated group nap, and those of us out and about were encouraged to do the same.

And from a cultural standpoint, I loved Italians. Their bronze, sun-kissed skin, animated expressions, and rich, romantic language endeared me to them instantly.

At dusk, we indulged in one last splurge and hired a gondola because, really, how can you visit Venice and *not* partake in the signature Venice experience? Our driver, Marco, was hilarious. He entertained us with stories about memorable passengers, such as the Harley-Davidson model who'd stripped naked as they cruised the canals, overcome with love for the city (and too much *prosecco*), and the numerous marriage proposals (and proposals gone awry) he'd witnessed. I liked Marco—you could tell that he enjoyed people and genuinely loved his job. We learned that in order to become a gondola driver, you had to go to school for three years to learn all the languages you needed to speak and the rules for steering the boat. Gondoliers also had to buy their own boats, which cost around 27,000 euro and needed to be replaced every three years. A 45-minute gondola ride cost between 70-100 euro, and most gondoliers made enough during the summer months (aka tourist season) to support their families through the winter.

As social and engaging as Marco was, he didn't talk our ears off for the whole ride—which I appreciated. This gave the four of us time to really soak in the moment, a once-in-a-lifetime event that could never, ever be replicated.

The gondola whisked us away from the heavily congested waterways into the intricate "back streets" of Venice, narrow canals where the water lapped right up against the back doors of homes. I leaned back against Damion's chest, his arms encircling my waist. I spent a fair amount of time obsessing about what was going to happen, but this was a development I never could have foreseen, especially given the Tony situation. Yet here we were, falling in love… It would be interesting to see what life was like when it was just the two of us. After we came off the road and settled into a routine, would it still feel like this? Did the magic have staying power?

I shook off the anxious thoughts. We still had 48 hours of perfect left. Foolish to waste it.

Gliding across the shimmery, moonlight-streaked pool, I was struck by my first regret of the trip. We should have spent more time in Italy. From the texture of mozzerella atop a vine-ripened tomato, to the heartwarming sight of an elderly couple sharing a bench as they fed the birds, I was once again reminded of the beauty in the simple things. I could have spent weeks in Italy, blissfully immersing myself in all things Italian, learning to speak the language. But the sad fact was, the money had run out. After this last hurrah, we would be escorting Faby down to Rome so she could fly home. Then Damion and I would head back to London to explore the next phase of our relationship.

Chapter Twenty-Nine

Damion

We spent Faby's last day in Europe on the road, making the five-hour trek from Venice to Rome. Due to our extended stay at the Fritz family hostel in Switzerland, the Italy leg of the girl's trip had been practically eliminated. Samantha's disappointment was palpable, but I promised her we'd return after I'd built up the monetary reserves. Now that she'd agreed to stay behind with me, we had plenty of time for further exploration.

We arrived at our hostel in Rome with about five hours of daylight left. After checking in and dropping our bags, we hit the town, trying to see as many sights as possible on our final day together. Since Faby was very serious about her faith, the Vatican was our first stop.

I'm not a religious guy, but the churches over here were something else. The designs and architecture were so awe-inspiring, God *must* have had a hand in their creation. How else could you explain the colorful mosaics that adorned the walls of St. Peter's Basillica?

I took a deep breath and tried to get in tune with the stillness that surrounded me. Removed from the frantic pace and pressures of the outside world, the space felt holy and sacred, a true sanctuary of timelessness. As I stood beside Samantha in the pew, my head bowed in quiet contemplation, I was overcome by gratitude for all that had transpired in the past month. It was truly a miracle that Fate had brought Samantha to London and opened her heart to me... I was feeling pretty damn blessed.

Afterwards we cruised by the Colosseum, so Faby could at least lay eyes on the famous monument. Then we grabbed dinner at a pizzeria, gelato to go, and posted up on the Spanish Steps for our final people-watching session.

"I just want to thank you guys for taking time out of your lives to accompany me on this journey," Faby said. She held JP's hand tight in hers. "Thanks to your fantastic company, this trip has far exceeded all expectations."

"It's been life-changing, for sure," I added. "Thank *you*, Fab, for giving us the opportunity to come together and share this experience. I will always look back on this summer as one of the highlights of my life."

"Me, too," JP said. "I am very grateful for the time I've had with all of you, my new American friends." His eyes never left Faby's face. "You will always have a place to stay in Brienz if you ever return." He smiled. "And I hope that you will."

To help with the fulfillment of that prophecy, we headed over to the Trevi Fountain. With our arms entwined, we approached the epic sculpture, which featured the god Neptune at the center. Then we took turns tossing a coin over our shoulder into the fountain, a gesture that, according to legend, ensured a return trip to Rome.

There were a lot of tears at the airport the next morning when we dropped Faby off. It was hard to believe that it had been three weeks since the girls had shown up on my doorstep. As great adventures do, this trip had changed all of our lives.

I'll admit, it was hard to watch Faby and JP say goodbye. We all knew this might be the last time they saw each other, and the intensity of that moment wasn't lost on any of us. Having to walk away from someone you cared about was the worst, and though Faby was trying to put on a brave front, I could tell she was just barely holding it together. I felt for her—if Samantha was getting on that plane, I'd probably be just as distraught. But thankfully, saying goodbye to Samantha was not scheduled to happen anytime soon.

JP flew back to Paris a few hours after Faby left. Like me, he had put numerous obligations on hold to run off with the girls, and it was time for him to return to reality. Samantha and I decided to stay one more night in Rome before starting our multi-day rail trip back to London.

This was my first time in Rome and I was diggin' it. The bustling metropolis was alive with tourists, traffic, and commerce; it could easily take a week to see all the notable attractions. I found the remnants from ancient civilizations fascinating; I couldn't believe the Colosseum still stood. *Gladiator* was one of my all-time favorite movies and it was surreal to stand inside the weathered arena, gazing upon the site where legit gladiators had fought to the death almost 2000 years ago. Powerful stuff.

Considering the battles that accompanied the fall of the Roman Empire in the 3rd century, the endurance of these ancient structures was humbling. We spent the afternoon wandering through the Roman Forum, which looked like an archaeological dig in progress. The site was littered with ruins from ancient Rome's equivalent of Capitol Hill. Being in the presence of a millenia worth of history was a historian's dream.

We paused at the remains of the Temple of Caesar, where Julius Caesar had been cremated after his assassination in 44 BC. "I have mad respect for Caesar," I mused, as I tried to picture the funeral pyre I'd read about in so many books. "He was a true visionary and laid the foundation for the Roman Empire."

"It's a shame he had to go out the way he did... murdered by his best friends and trusted confidants." Samantha shook her head. "To have your last moments filled with such betrayal—what an awful way to go."

"But history made him immortal," I said. "Very few people are able to make a contribution whose impact persists through generations, much less eras. I mean, even today, they are still making films about the man. Telling his story. Now that's what I call a legacy."

I admit, I had Caesar-like aspirations. I definitely wanted to make my mark and change the course of history. I felt very strongly that it was every person's responsibility to leave this world (or their corner of the world), a little better than when they found it. My personal passion was increasing black male life expectancy, but instead of focusing on small scale, individual transformation, I was trying to figure out how to ignite the next great social movement and create a new wave of activist leaders. My thoughts returned to my research, which had been simmering on the back burner for weeks. There were still so many interviews to conduct and coalitions to meet with. As great as this trip had been, I wasn't going to be able to change the world unless I got back to work.

Chapter Thirty

Samantha

Truth be told, I never felt at home in London. While it was great playing house with Damion and getting my wifey on, after two months of cohabitation, the initial excitement of being in a new place wore off and that all-too-familiar restlessness returned. With school back in session, Damion was teaching two classes and spending a lot of time at the University. I spent many afternoons sitting on the deck in his flat, staring at the traffic on the street below. Everyone had somewhere to go, something to do. Except me. My job was to sit idle on plastic patio furniture, a spectator of life. I needed to figure out what I was going to do with myself.

Most would envy me, I'm sure. Living abroad, with no job to tie me down or suck up my time, supported and taken care of by my handsome and attentive lover—it was a charmed life. And while some women wanted nothing more than to find a man to take care of them, I was not comfortable with this level of dependence. This was Damion's path, Damion's dream. When was I going to find my own distinct calling? There had to be more to life than keeping Damion company.

"Just start applying for stuff," Damion said, as we enjoyed dinner out in the West End. "See what kinds of offers you get and go from there."

"But where? I still can't decide if I want to go back to LA, stay here with you, or try out an entirely new city. And besides, what is the point of applying for stuff in the States? It's not like I'm available for interviews at the moment."

"You gotta have faith, Sam. Just set some things in motion and let the forward momentum of the Universe take over. You're anxious because you feel like you're standing still. You need to make some moves." He paused. "Maybe it *is* time to head home."

I looked up from the grilled chicken salad I'd been picking at. *Well, that wasn't the response I'd been expecting.* His words stung. This was the first time Damion had suggested I leave. Had I overstayed my welcome?

"Oh, well, sure. I can go home. If that's what you want."

"Now, stop that." He took my hand. "You know the last thing I *want* is to send you away. But I don't want to hold you back, either. I get that you have your own mountain to climb. I'm just trying to help you get to the top."

This was probably what I loved most about Damion—he never tried to impose his will, desires, or preferences on me. I was a pretty stubborn individual, and even at my most indecisive, I cringed whenever someone tried to tell me what to do. His ability to respect this key facet of my personality was one of the reasons we got along so well.

Instead of trying to steer me toward a particular course of action, Damion's role had always been to present options, and then play sounding board as I talked through said options. But this exercise had a different dimension now that we were "in a relationship." Before, he could offer me advice as an objective third party. But now, I was acutely aware of the fact that any decision I made would impact him. When he said things like, "Maybe it's time to head home," was there a subtext in there that I should be paying attention to?

"Hey, isn't that Reinarman?" Damion asked, pointing toward the patio.

I turned to look. Chuck Reinarman, one of my Sociology professors from UCSC, was being seated at a table across from a stunning blond.

"Wow, that *is* him. This world is too small."

Dr. Reinarman was pretty much a rock star as far as professors go. I took three classes with him while at UCSC, and would have taken more if he hadn't been on leave during my final two quarters. His specialty was drugs and drug policy, and he was a vocal proponent of some rather controversial agendas, such as the legalization of marijuana. This made him super cool amongst undergrads, and his signature course, "Drugs in Society," was one of the most popular on campus. He was also super accessible to students, down-to-earth, and wildly charismatic. I knew several girls with mad crushes on him, despite the significant age difference.

"You should go say hi," Damion said.

I shook my head. "I don't want to bother him. I'm sure he doesn't even remember me."

Damion frowned. "Samantha Merrick, have you learned nothing from the *Celestine Prophecy*? You just came across one of your professors from Santa Cruz in a restaurant in *London*. I'm sorry, but that is too much of a coincidence to not act on it."

He had a point. I mean, what were the odds?

I walked over to Chuck's table. Not only did he remember me, but he was so intrigued by my random appearance that he invited me and Damion to join him and his date.

Turns out Chuck was on a sabbatical from UCSC, and had spent the past six months doing research in Amsterdam, of all places.

"Oh, I'm so jealous," I gushed at the mention of my European happy place. "I *love* Amsterdam. I could totally see myself living there."

"I had the same reaction the first time I visited," Chuck said. "One of the best investments I ever made was buying property in Amsterdam. My apartment is in a fantastic location, so it's easy to market as a short-term/vacation rental to generate income. And whenever I want to come and spend some time, I always have somewhere to stay."

My eyes grew wide. "You actually own a place in Amsterdam?"

"Yes. I travel to the Netherlands regularly for research and leisure. I hope to retire there one day. It just made sense."

"Wow."

"You know, Inga and I will be traveling to Istanbul next week before I head back to the States, and my next tenant isn't moving in until December. You're more than welcome to stay at my place if you like."

My jaw practically slapped the table. "Are you serious? How much would you charge for a couple of weeks?"

He waved his hand. "I don't need your money. Save it for your student loans."

I pinched myself under the table. This was not actually happening. Chuck Reinarman was not sitting here offering me somewhere to stay, rent-free, in Amsterdam. Damion, who was rarely rendered speechless, looked just as stunned as I was.

"Wow, that is incredibly generous of you, Dr. Rein—"

"Please, call me Chuck."

"Okay. That is super generous of you, Chuck, and I am definitely interested. But you have to let me give you something." Though I only had a couple hundred dollars to my name, this was a non-negotiable as far as I was concerned. My mama taught me that when it comes to men, there is no such thing as something for nothing.

Chuck leaned back in his chair, stroking his thick beard. "Alright, let's see. How about we work out a trade? I have some interviews I need transcribed. You help me with the transcriptions, and I'll let you stay at my place for a few weeks. Win-win. How does that sound?"

I was starting to see why my classmates crushed so hard on this man. He was like a super-handsome fairy godfather, swooping in to save the day.

The thought of relocating to Amsterdam invigorated me. This was movement, a mission, a much-needed catalyst to free me from my current state of stagnation. The hand of Fate at work. Where would *this* road lead?

Running into Chuck at that restaurant was probably the greatest stroke of luck I'd encountered thus far.

Damion and I traveled back to Amsterdam the following weekend. Chuck owned a modest, one bedroom apartment, small but comfortable, in the heart of the Jordaan, my favorite neighborhood in Amsterdam. Within an hour of my return, I felt better; not just happy to be back, but happy in my soul. I no longer felt directionless, flailing through life like a busted satellite through the atmosphere. Having this opportunity fall into my lap renewed my faith in the Universe. My faith that things would work themselves out if I just let go…

After a great weekend experiencing Amsterdam as lovers, Damion had to leave. Though it was only four hours by train from London to Amsterdam, Damion probably wouldn't be able to come down very often because of his teaching schedule. I was actually fine with the time apart; I was looking forward to the solitude, the perfect opportunity to engage in some no-holds-barred heart to hearts with my authentic self. I wasn't anxious about the uncertainty anymore. I was excited to figure out my next steps, confident that the correct path forward would eventually reveal itself to me.

Not to mention the fantastic Amsterdam weed I'd have at my disposal to help the process along.

Chapter Thirty- One

Damion

I'm not gonna lie—coming home to an empty apartment after nearly three months with Samantha was a sobering moment. We'd just come off an incredible journey and were starting to build a life together, melding and merging in every way. There was so much magic surrounding us that I felt like we were living in an alternate reality. Her absence was disorienting. She had taken the magic with her and left me behind in the lonely, responsibility-ridden, real world.

Thankfully, there was still plenty of her stuff around the apartment, assurance that she would return. A camisole hung in the bathroom; a hairbrush lay on the nightstand. When I crawled into bed, the pillowcases were still soaked in her scent, for which I was grateful. It helped ease the ache.

But as much as I missed her, the break was probably the best thing for both of us. Samantha needed to do some soul-searching and I had plenty on my plate. The fall semester was underway at Goldsmiths and I was teaching two courses—a seminar on the Civil Rights Movement and a larger lecture on the African American Experience. Preparing for lectures and grading papers was pretty time-consuming, and it was nice to be able to devote my full attention to the task. The privilege of educating and opening young minds was a charge I took very seriously.

My impromptu jaunt around Europe had also put me behind on my research. With my dissertation completed, I was embarking on a whole new project. I'd spent the past year researching UK youth movements and vigilante groups, and had hours worth of interviews to sort through before I could start writing. The goal was to produce a draft of a publishable manuscript by the time my postdoc was up. If I could manage that, I was a shoo-in for a position my mentor, Professor Schiller, was grooming me for. Here in London.

Samantha and I had been skirting the issue of what to do about our relationship long-term, focusing instead on living in the moment. But I still had some time left on my postdoc, and was very interested in the prospect of taking a job out here. Would Samantha entertain the idea of permanently relocating to London?

As I relaxed on the couch grading papers, I was startled by a knock at the front door. *What the…* Had Samantha decided to surprise me with a midweek visit?

I was greeted by Taja's shapely form posed in the doorway. She was rocking the hell out of some skintight jeans, a sheer gold blouse, and her trademark leather jacket. However, the sexiest thing she had on was the "Come here, I want to devour you" look on her face. She clutched a bottle of merlot in her left hand.

"What's up, Taj?"

After planting a kiss on my cheek, she pushed past me into the apartment, not waiting to be invited in. "I heard your friend left."

I shut the door. "What, you been staking me out?"

"What can I say, good news travels fast." She set the wine on the counter and removed her jacket. I could see the curves of her ample cleavage beneath the thin fabric. "I'm actually here to give you shit," she said. "You haven't been to a meeting since the semester started."

Taja was referring to UpStart, a coalition she had co-founded that brought together activists and educators to collaborate on social justice projects. The group was building a critical mass of support, and with an influx of funds, they could widen their reach and triple their impact. The current focus was on grant writing, and all hands were supposed to be on deck.

I bowed my head—Taja had succeeded in shaming me. "I know. I've been playing catch up since I got home."

"Well, now that your distraction is gone, maybe we can get you back on track. I've missed you, D." She ran her fingernails along the flesh of my forearm.

I shifted so I was out of her reach. "Samantha is not a distraction, she's my girlfriend. And she'll be back. She just went down to Amsterdam for a few weeks."

"I thought she was just *visiting* from the States?"

"She is… But she's in transition. Still trying to figure out her next steps."

Taja opened the bottle of wine she'd brought. "Interesting."

"What's interesting?"

157

She poured us each a glass. "Your choice in mates. You're such a visionary, so ambitious. I always assumed you'd gravitate toward someone with similar qualities. Not someone who was still 'figuring things out.' "

I took the glass she offered me. "Ooh, is that a twinge of jealousy I detect? I thought you made it a point not to get attached."

"Trust me, I am not jealous of the little American girl," she said. "I am concerned about my friend. I have seen many freedom fighters abandon the struggle because of family obligations or some woman." Her voice rose to match the passion of her conviction. "Your mission on this earth is greater than that of your self. Any partner who is not on this mission with you has the ability to pull you off the path."

"Samantha has no intention of pulling me off my path," I argued.

"Oh no? Well, let me ask you this, friend. What happens when Samantha returns to the U.S.? Will you follow her?"

I took a gulp of wine. I certainly hadn't expected the evening to devolve into an interrogation.

"I don't know."

"Uh huh. The fact that you don't know is the first sign of trouble. When was the last time you were unclear about your next step? That position at Oxford is yours if you want it—how in the world could you contemplate leaving the UK right now? Who walks away from an opportunity like that?"

Of course, she was right, which is why I was so uncomfortable all of a sudden. I refilled my glass.

"I'm not walking away from anything, including Samantha. People negotiate successful long-distance relationships all the time."

"Yes, but is that really how you want to spend your time? Pining and missing someone?"

"Point taken. Now is this the only reason you stopped by, to bust my balls?"

She smiled. "Ah, I've always loved that expression. Actually, I have missed our talks. Sergei is no sparring partner. He doesn't have any ideas of his own; he just agrees with everything I say and lets me dominate the conversation. He's either afraid of me, or trying to get in my pants."

Probably both, I thought.

"If he wants to get in your pants, he's going about it all wrong," I said with a wink. Taja loved nothing more than an anger fuck after a spirited debate.

"As I said, he is no match for me." She rested her hand on my thigh. "Any chance you and Samantha have an open relationship?"

I laughed. "Nope. I'm very much off the market."

Her hand inched closer to my package, which began to stir. "You sure? Not even one last fling for old time's sake? I promise I won't tell."

I shook my head as I removed her hand from my lap. "Tempting... but no."

Taja finished her wine and stood. "Oh well, it was worth a try." Grabbing her jacket, she fixed me with a stern glare. "I better see you at the meeting on Thursday or I'll be back."

"Yes, ma'am."

She blew me a kiss and let herself out. The woman was like a tornado—she tore through a room and left chaos in her wake. I'd always been so amused watching her in action, but being at the epicenter of such a thorough dismantling of my previously held beliefs was not a pleasant experience. I was shaken and confused, surrounded by a pile of emotional debris.

Taja was right—I'd been avoiding the tough questions about the practical realities of my future with Samantha. My blind faith was probably a bit naïve. I knew Samantha better than anyone; she was a flight risk. Would I end up as a case of "out of sight, out of mind" when she returned to the States without me? Could she remain faithful if we had to spend months or years apart? Could she trust that I was keeping my end of the bargain, or would every conversation be an interrogation of my comings and goings?

I poured myself another glass of wine. Something told me the honeymoon was about to be over.

Chapter Thirty-Two

Samantha

The month I spent in Amsterdam was a blissful time in my life, punctuated by moments of wonder and delightful synchronicity. I'd never experienced anything like it—things consistently going *right*. Took some getting used to, but eventually I settled into a state that could only be described as...happiness.

What I learned from floating in this uninterrupted stream of happiness was that joy and anxiety could not coexist, and it was entirely my choice which of the two would dominate. The mind is powerful, and when you focus on the negative, the hardships and struggles take center stage. But the exact same thing happens when you focus on the positive—all your blessings and opportunities become apparent. Armed with this epiphany, I was seeing the world through a shiny, new perspective. Even my reflections on the most painful times in my life lacked their usual sting.

I thought about Tony a lot as I wandered the streets of Amsterdam. The last time I felt this kind of pure, unfiltered magic

161

was during the early part of our relationship, before everything went so terribly wrong. I didn't think I'd ever be able to recapture that sense of childlike wonder—I figured I was too jaded. But Damion was teaching me that a heart could indeed heal, and through the healing process I was starting to let go of some of the Tony stuff that I was still, after all this time, holding on to. It was nice to be able to think of him and have it not hurt.

Forward progress, indeed.

In addition to being genuinely happy, I was also ridiculously productive. I devoted a few hours each day to interview transcriptions, and really enjoyed the work. Chuck's latest project contributed to the growing body of research supporting the legalization of marijuana, and he had interviewed legislators, policymakers, and coffee shop owners here in Amsterdam in an attempt to proactively address any implementation issues the United States might face on its way to progressive reform. Since I was supportive of the initiative, the tedious task of transcribing hours of interviews became an enriching learning experience. I got through all the interviews in a week's time, which earned me Chuck's admiration and gratitude, along with a small bonus for being so speedy with my work.

Like most academics, Chuck had an extensive book collection, and with the transcriptions completed and nothing but time on my hands, I was able to do quite a bit of reading. I tore through Angela Davis's autobiography, and enjoyed Richard Wright's *Native Son* for the first time. I also read both books that Chuck had authored, as well as his numerous journal articles and essays. My admiration for him swelled as I became intimately acquainted with his work.

Not only had Chuck shaped his field, he had affected drug policy at the state and federal level, even providing expert testimony at congressional hearings. He was so humble and down-to-earth, I never could have imagined the extent of his reach.

All that reading reactivated the academic side of my brain as I recalled the joy I felt when I was conducting my own research. I had a sincere passion for inquiry; by studying social problems, people had the potential to enact social change. This was a core value of mine, one I shared with Damion, but while he pursued his goals, I was sitting on my hands, pouting. With so many social issues that needed to be addressed, there was no excuse for letting my skills, talents, and research training languish.

This burst of clarity led me to seek out Mariana again. Not for sex, but for more conversation. I ventured into the Red Light District one night and found Mariana in her regular window. She remembered me, and seemed happy to see me. I let her know I was going to be in town for a few weeks, and asked if I could buy her lunch sometime. To my surprise and delight, she accepted.

My date with Mariana ended up being the start of a really awesome friendship. She introduced me to her daughter, Eva, and her closest girlfriends (some sex workers, some not), and I was invited to hang out often. I felt fortunate to stumble upon a sister circle here in Amsterdam, as there really is no substitute for the counsel of women when you're in the midst of a major life transition.

This collection of working girls, single moms, and entrepreneurs really helped me appreciate the instinctual nature of female self-sufficiency. Some of my new friends had fled truly deplorable circumstances in their native countries, but had turned things around here in Amsterdam. To them, prostitution represented a pathway to a better life, a stepping stone rather than a last resort. I learned so much from them about perseverance in the face of adversity.

Being around those less fortunate also put things into perspective. I'd adopted a helpless victim stance in regard to my current predicament, engaging in self-pity and bemoaning my lack of direction. But this attitude ignored my position of privilege. I had options available to me, options my new friends would give anything to have. I owed it to these ladies, and women across the globe, to leverage my position in support of women's rights. Maybe that was my calling.

I started spending time at the Prostitute Information Center (PIC). The women there were doing amazing work to improve the quality of life for sex workers in the city. Though prostitution was not legal in most of the United States, the sex industry was still thriving, and women on the streets lacked access to basic services. Could I instigate reform around the culture of prostitution in the U.S. the way Dr. Reinarman was trying to ignite the movement to decriminalize marijuana?

Damion was so excited to hear about my various breakthroughs when he came to visit. We were hanging out at my favorite coffee shop, La Tertulia, and I had been talking nonstop about Mariana, the girls, and the flashes of inspiration they had triggered.

"Wow, you're like a completely different person," he remarked, a wide grin plastered across his face. "I've never seen you so energized."

"I know. The past few weeks have been amazing. I need to figure out a way to get back into research. And definitely pursue Grad School. But I don't want to wait a whole year to get back in the game—I need to capitalize on my intellectual momentum. Do you know of anyone at Goldsmiths, working on women's issues, who needs a Research Assistant? I would even be open to volunteering if there aren't any paid positions available, anything to keep me busy and engaged."

"I will definitely ask around," Damion said. "That sounds like a great plan."

It was a great plan, and one I felt good about. Staying in London with Damion could definitely work if I could find something worthwhile to do with my time.

Chapter Thirty-Three

Damion

Samantha returned to London on November 30, and two weeks later Goldsmiths broke for winter recess. Classes did not resume until mid-January. I was happy to have Samantha with me for the holidays, as spending Christmas alone last year had been pretty depressing. But this Christmas would more than make up for it if everything went as planned.

I'd decided to ask Samantha to marry me.

Yes, it was fast; we hadn't even hit our six-month anniversary. But the time we'd spent together had been magical and what can I say—when you know, you know. I was ready to get a head start on forever.

Of course my impending proposition generated a fair share of nerves. There was always a chance she may say no. But I was feeling pretty confident. Things between us were solid, and Samantha was planning to apply to Grad Schools here in London. Not the actions of a woman who wasn't committed. It was my turn to signal that I was also in this for the long haul.

I found the perfect ring while Samantha was in Amsterdam. I popped into this antique store on a whim one day, and this piece of jewelry caught my eye. Samantha was not into "bling," and the sapphire and diamonds arranged in the shape of a flower, set in white gold, was striking and unique—just like Samantha. The setting even garnered Faby's seal of approval; she'd responded with support, excitement, and enthusiasm when I sent her a picture of it. All I had to do was plan the perfect proposal.

Men are notorious for being substandard in the romance department, but I found it pretty easy to be romantic when I had the right inspiration. Samantha was also really easy to plan for because she was pretty low-maintenance and genuinely appreciative of the simple things. She gave more weight to the sentiment behind a gesture than the cost or level of extravagance. But still, I wanted the moment I proposed to be a memorable one. A day neither of us would ever forget.

My mentor, Dr. Schiller, had a vacation home in the Cotswalds, about two hours outside of London. When he learned of my intention to propose, he suggested I take Samantha to his cabin. I took him up on his offer; Samantha and I had yet to venture into the English countryside, and it would be great to get out of the city for a bit.

Dr. Schiller's home was amazing—a four-bedroom cottage on the outskirts of Stroud. We had a lovely Christmas in the country, visiting the neighboring towns, exploring the numerous walking trails, and making love in front of a roaring fireplace. I enjoyed this glimpse of what life with Samantha would be like when we were married, with a home of our own. It felt right.

The night before we headed back to Brixton, I cooked up a feast for us—steak, roasted potatoes, and steamed broccoli. Samantha loved it when I cooked for her, as cooking was not exactly her forte. My goal had been to serve up a solid week of the queen's treatment, culminating in my grand proposal. So far, everything was going as planned.

"So, I have a little present for you," I said, after we finished loading the dishwasher.

Samantha frowned. "Damion, I thought we agreed to forgo Christmas presents this year. You're not allowed to discard the rules like that."

"I know. But if you accept my gift, it will technically be a present for both of us."

"But..."

"Always with the buts." I set the tiny box on the table in front of her. "Just open it."

She flipped the lid up and gasped. "Oh my... wow." Her eyes widened with surprise. "This is beautiful."

I assumed the position, dropping down to one knee before her. "Samantha, I've loved you for a long time. You embody everything I want in a partner. Being with you stimulates my mind and nourishes my soul. You make me feel boundless, but also keep me grounded. You're my best friend, my lover, and a kick-ass travel companion. I want you by my side for the rest of my journeys." I took deep breath. "Would you do me the great honor of becoming my wife?"

She was shaking her head in shock, disbelief coloring her expression. "This is... I'm just... oh my god—you're serious?

You're really asking me to marry you?"

"I am really asking you to marry me." I flashed a nervous smile. "So, what do you say?"

She dropped to her knees as well. "I love you, Dame. So much."

I swallowed, my confidence starting to waver. The way her voice trailed off... Was there another 'but' coming?

"I've never had someone like you in my corner," she said softly. "I've never felt so safe. I trust you with my heart, hell, I trust you with my life. I can't imagine doing any of this without you either. So... yes." She smiled. "I will marry you."

Chapter Thirty-Four

Samantha

The new year certainly started off on a high note. What an unbelievable turn of events. Me, engaged? I had left the U.S. six months ago and touched down in an alternate universe, a land of love and happily ever after. This was the most foreign territory I'd ever traversed, but much to my surprise, I liked it. In fact, I was thriving. Being with Damion was the easiest, most natural thing in the world. If he wanted to spend the rest of his life honoring and cherishing me, who was I to say no?

When we returned to London, I kicked my plan to find work into high gear—I was done freeloading. However, when I went to inquire about applying for a work visa, our grand plans hit a brick wall. Not only was I ineligible for a work visa, but I had almost reached the limit on my tourist visa. The UK only allowed foreigners to stay in the country for up to six months; I would need to head back to the U.S. before January 22nd.

Just like that, my "happily ever after" and "meant to be" balloons deflated. I had finally figured out what I wanted to do, and who I wanted to do it with, and the Universe was telling me no. Sending me back to square one. Even worse, it was sending me back to *Los Angeles.*

This was a terrible sign.

I left the visa service center and headed for the nearest bar to grab a drink (or four) before catching the Tube back to Brixton. This sucked. Damion was building a life here—would his plans change when he found out I couldn't stay with him? I didn't want him to alter his course on my account, which I was almost certain he would offer to do. Damion's devotion to me was total, which I appreciated, but I hated the thought of holding him back. His dreams were just as valid as mine.

This really sucked.

I took a seat at the bar beside a dark-skinned woman in her mid-40s. As two brown-skinned Americans on foreign soil, we were drawn into conversation naturally. Carolyn Ford, an entertainment attorney from Los Angeles, was also having a bad day. She was in town to negotiate a rather lucrative distribution deal for one of her clients, and after hours of presentations for a parade of suited men, enduring the most condescending questions, she had left without settling on terms. Carolyn was posted up at the bar, in an even worse mood than I was, consoling herself with vodka martinis.

"I didn't encounter one woman today who wasn't a secretary or clerk, and I'm pretty sure I was the only woman of color in the entire building," she vented.

"That's lame," I said, sharing her frustration.

"Really lame." She drained her glass and ordered another. "They thought they could bully me into submission. I'd rather leave the deal on the table than let those assholes lowball my client."

I'd heard this lament before. My sister, Megan, who was also climbing the corporate ladder in Southern California, often complained about the lack of women in the workplace, especially in upper management. But as Megan and Carolyn could attest, even if you managed to crack the glass ceiling, it was lonely at the top because women often failed to command the respect they deserved from their male counterparts.

"I feel for you," I said. "Negotiating with people who flaunt their privilege must be so aggravating. That's why women should start their own businesses, so we don't have to deal with this nonsense."

"You sound like my sister, Cassandra," Carolyn said with a smile. "She refuses to operate in a man's world. A few years ago she started a company to support and promote female business owners in Los Angeles. She wanted to create networks where women of color could locate and collaborate with each other, a web of professional sisterhood and empowerment."

"That's what I'm talking about!" I said, eager to hear more. "I've always believed that the key to success is collectivity, not competition. But I think that most women, Black women in particular, are so used to doing everything themselves that they forget to ask for help. Leaning on someone and showing what may be perceived as weakness is almost counterintuitive. We struggle needlessly in solitude."

"Exactly. The irony is, Cassandra's trying to build this empire to help other women, but she isn't able to progress as quickly as she'd like because she lacks the resources she hopes to cultivate."

"How big is the company?" I asked. "Does she have staff?"

"She has four employees, two of them part-time. Cassandra *had* a full-time assistant, but she quit a few weeks ago and left things in total disarray. Cassandra has such vision, but she's not the most organized person. I help as much as I can, but I have my own practice to manage."

The wheels in my head were turning. This was another one of those serendipitous coincidences that felt... fated. "Has your sister found a new assistant?" I asked.

"Thanks to her current state of overwhelm, she hasn't even posted a job ad yet. Why, do you know someone who's looking for work?"

I gave Carolyn a rundown of my educational background, interests, and long-term goals. She was impressed by my passion, and listened intently as I described the research I'd done at UCSC on sex trafficking, and the work I wanted to do to improve the quality of life for sex workers.

"When do you plan to return to the States?" she asked.

"I'll be heading back to LA in a few weeks," I replied.

Carolyn handed me a business card. "Send me your résumé and I'll put you in touch with my sister," she said with a smile.

As soon as I got back to the flat, I hopped online and started Googling Carolyn and Cassandra Ford. The Internet was full of articles about the numerous accomplishments of the Ford sisters.

Carolyn was the product of Stanford Law School, and one of the most sought-after attorneys in the entertainment industry. Her client list was filled with A-list celebrities and media moguls. Cassandra had gone the less lucrative, social services route, and was considered a pillar of the community. Her company, OWN It (of which Carolyn was a silent partner), provided small business counseling for female entrepreneurs, everything from courses on accounting to assistance with grant-writing.

OWN It's mission statement resonated in the halls of my heart:

Don't just take charge of your destiny; **OWN It**.

Pages of testimonials chronicled Cassandra's impact, the hundreds of lives she'd changed by empowering women to turn their dreams into tangible products. Smiling, successful faces beamed back at me from the website.

This was what I wanted to do with my life.

I was beyond inspired. However, I could see what Carolyn meant when she talked about the lack of organization. OWN It had an important mission, but the company's web presence was anemic. Cassandra wasn't taking advantage of all the technology at her disposal to further her cause. With the right infrastructure, such as a message board where members could share advice and resources, OWN It could dramatically expand its reach. An active, engaged member base and virtual community could take OWN It's message nationwide.

I poured all my ideas into a cover letter, describing how impacted I'd been by her vision, and the different ways I felt her work could be built upon. By the time Damion got home, I'd pounded out five pages on his laptop.

"Damn, girl—you cranked this out in one afternoon?" he asked when he finished reading my proposal.

"What can I say, I was hit by a flash of inspiration. What do you think?"

"I like it. Very innovative. Clear and articulate presentation. Your passion really shines through. And the company sounds great—I couldn't have created a more perfect position for you. I hope you get it."

"Me, too." I'd been pacing, propelled back and forth across the hardwood floor by nerves. I finally exhaled and took a seat beside him. "I can't believe I have to leave."

"I know. But if you get this gig, at least you'll have something to look forward to and be excited about. This is a fantastic opportunity."

As great as it was to have his full support, I was a little hurt that he wasn't experiencing a more dramatic form of separation anxiety. "But what about us?" I said softly. I lowered my eyes, embarrassed and horrified by how pathetic I sounded.

Damion's face softened. "There will *always* be an us, Sam. Believe that. We'll figure it out."

I was so thankful to have a man in my life who was so unconditionally supportive. Damion always had my best interests in the forefront of his mind. *This* is what love was supposed to look like. While Damion fixed dinner, I put the finishing touches on my résumé and proposal, then emailed the entire packet to Carolyn Ford. Caution was officially in the wind.

I had just nodded off when Damion's phone rang. He slipped out of bed to answer as I glanced at the clock. Two a.m.

"Yes, she's right here." Damion handed me the phone. "It's for you."

It was Cassandra Ford. She had just read my email.

"I know it's late there," she began, after identifying herself. "I hope I didn't wake you."

I sat up in bed. "No, Ms. Ford, it's fine. I'm happy to hear from you."

"Please, call me Cassie." Her voice flowed over the line with warmth and familiarity, as if we were old friends. "I'd like to speak with you about this beautiful proposal you sent to my sister, Carolyn."

It took me a minute to realize I was actually awake and this was *actually* happening. Ms. Ford was heaping buckets of praise upon me, beginning with how highly her sister spoke of me, and how impressed they'd both been with my ideas for the company. As Cassandra described to me her vision for OWN It, I was surprised by how intuitively I'd been able to tap into it. Though we'd never met, somehow we were totally in sync.

"I've been struggling with all this technology stuff," Cassandra explained. "I don't like computers. To be frank, I don't understand them and don't care to learn. My assistant used to handle that stuff and now that she's gone, I have no idea how to navigate all these systems she set up. I don't know the difference between a database and a directory."

I laughed. "Well, I could definitely help you with all that."

"Yes, I'm sure you could. Which is why I'm so anxious to meet with you. When will you be back in Los Angeles?"

I paused. This was a serious job prospect, my *only* prospect, and I felt the need to jump on it. I couldn't risk her giving the job to someone else. "I can be in LA by the end of the week," I blurted out.

"Wonderful," Cassandra said. "I'd like to meet with you as soon as you get back."

I gave Damion the thumbs up sign as I bounced up and down on the edge of the bed, a huge grin plastered on my face. "I look forward to it, Ms. Ford."

"Me, too. I'll email you some dates and times that I'm available to meet. Safe travels, my dear. I'll see you soon."

Chapter Thirty-Five

Damion

With mixed emotions, I listened to Samantha recount her conversation with Cassandra Ford. This was an amazing opportunity—no denying that. Ms. Ford was doing great work in Los Angeles to assist women of color in realizing their dreams and aspirations. Everything about OWN It was fully in line with Samantha's values, politics, and passions; that it was all going down in Los Angeles—near her closest friends and family—was the icing on the cake. Samantha could not let this moment pass her by. Even if that meant leaving London in *four days.*

Despite the whirlwind nature of it all, Samantha was giddy. Her trademark pessimism was nowhere to be found, and I don't think I'd ever seen her so excited about the future, which made me happy. And sad, because I wouldn't be there to share it with her.

Yeah, it would be hard not having her with me. This had been the best six months of my life; being separated by an ocean again was not something I was looking forward to. But I had no intention of trying to talk her out of it. I was not possessive by nature, so if her dreams led her away from me for a little bit, I was okay with that. When you love someone, you learn to put their needs ahead of your own. Samantha would have nothing but my love and support if she decided to head home.

"So, what do you think?" she asked. I could see in her eyes that she was nervous about my response.

"I think your prayers have been answered," I said with a smile. "This is about as close to your dream job as it gets."

"I know," she said. "I can't believe this is happening. And so fast."

"That's usually the way things go when they're meant to be," I said with a wink. "So… four days, huh?"

Samantha fell silent, her gaze fixed on the floor. "I'm so torn, Dame. Of course I want to rush home and meet with Cassandra before she changes her mind or finds someone else. But the thought of leaving you…"

Honestly, that was all I needed to hear to feel okay about things. Though she had accepted my proposal, it was still hard to tell sometimes if Samantha had really fallen for me the way I'd fallen for her. But I knew Sam—if she wasn't trying to be with me, she'd use this relocation as an out, a way to separate and end things without harming our friendship. But the look on her face told a different story. She was really upset about having to leave.

"Hey," I said, pulling her into my arms. "I love you. There is nothing you can do, no amount of distance, that will ever change that. We'll work this out. I'd ride to the end of the earth for you, girl, you know that."

"But I can't ask you to leave London…"

"You don't have to ask. I still plan on marrying you, and if me returning to the States at the end of my postdoc is what's best for *us,* I will gladly head back to Cali. Life without you doesn't compare to having you by my side. I'm down to do this, whatever it takes. Are you in?"

Samantha broke into a huge smile. "All in."

Chapter Thirty-Six

Samantha

Four days later, I was on a plane. LON to JFK to LAX. Saying goodbye to Damion was heart-wrenching, and I cried through most of the first leg of my flight. I felt silly for getting so emotional; after all, I would see him in six months after the semester ended. It's not like this was *goodbye*. But Damion was my safety blanket, and while I recognized how necessary this separation was for our professional development, I didn't want to be away from him. I knew from experience that missing someone can be paralyzing. Hopefully Damion's absence wouldn't impair my ability to function.

Time to see what this long-distance relationship stuff was all about.

OWN It was located on the second floor of an office building in Santa Monica. Sunlight poured through the large windows, illuminating recent issues of *Black Enterprise*, *Essence*, and *VIBE* stacked neatly on the coffee table. The soft trickle of a fountain provided a peaceful ambiance in the reception area, the vibe professional, but relaxed.

Though I was ten minutes early, I was promptly escorted back to Ms. Ford's office. Cassandra Ford bore a strong physical resemblance to her younger sister, but the similarity ended there. While Carolyn had been brisk and methodical in her tailored pant suit, Cassandra's colorful scarves, flowing skirt, and large, dramatic jewelry signaled a more carefree spirit. A piece of amber the size of my fist hung on a chain around her neck, and her waist-length dreadlocks were piled high atop her head in a makeshift crown. She greeted me with a warm hug, as if I were a long-lost niece or granddaughter rather than a job applicant. My fondness for her was instantaneous.

Before we got started, Cassandra took me on a tour. The nine-room suite was modest, but Cassandra had made excellent use of the space.

"There are two other staff members besides myself," Cassandra explained as she showed me the break room, conference room, and four large offices. "Lacey, my bookkeeper, works Monday through Wednesday, and a part-time paralegal from Carolyn's firm helps out with contracts. We also have two interns from UCLA working the front desk. They're responsible for fielding inquiries, scheduling, and outreach."

I followed her down the hall to the seminar room, which could comfortably seat thirty people around a large table.

"We host workshops and classes in here. Right now, we have drop-in small business counseling on Tuesdays and Saturdays.

About seven regulars also meet here on Sundays for an informal support group. My goal is to have this space utilized every night of the week."

"Can anyone rent the room?" I asked.

"Yes, as long as their programming supports OWN It's mission."

We concluded our tour and settled in Cassandra's office to chat over tea and pastries. I had expected a formal interview, perhaps before a panel of stakeholders, but it soon became clear that Cassandra's opinion was the only one that mattered, and she preferred a casual and intimate setting. Cassandra actually did most of the talking, sharing stories from the early days of OWN It. Before she had secured the investors and sponsors who made this all possible, Cassandra had run the company out of her garage. Given the company's humble beginnings, her trajectory was impressive; Cassandra's laser focus and fierce ambition reminded me a lot of Faby.

"So, what do you think?" Cassandra asked. We'd been conversing for about an hour, getting to know each other and sharing our goals for the future.

"I think your organization is amazing," I offered. "I would be honored to be part of it, in any capacity."

"Well, as you know, I'm anxious to fill the assistant position. I see a lot of potential in you, Ms. Merrick, and would be interested in having you start right away, on a trial basis. I can offer you twenty dollars an hour to start. At the end of the first month, if we're both happy with how things are going, we can re-negotiate your salary and bring you on as a permanent employee. A formal offer comes with access to benefits, and after your first year of employment, shares of the company."

"Shares of the company?"

"Yes, everyone with a long-term affiliation with OWN It is given a chance to become an investor or partner. I believe this model of shared responsibility will ensure the company's success."

My head was spinning. Benefits? Shares in OWN It? This was too good to be true.

"That all sounds wonderful, Ms. Ford. I can't tell you how grateful I am for this opportunity."

Cassandra extended her hand. "Welcome to OWN It, Samantha."

At the end of my first month, I'd succeeded in impressing Cassandra with my energy and initiative. Not only was I rewarded with the permanent position she'd promised, but I received a significant bump in pay. The salary was so high that I foolishly tried to decline her initial offer.

"That's a lot of money, Ms. Ford. I can live on half of that. Wouldn't the funds be better spent if we reinvested them in one of our programs?"

"Samantha," she scolded. "What is the mission of OWN It? Women helping women. Lesson One: Know your worth. You are doing fantastic work and bring a unique skill set to the table. Do you know what male IT staff and marketing mangers get paid in this town? Why shouldn't your salary be on par with your peers? I *am* making an investment, dear. I'm investing in you."

"Well, when you put it like that…"

"Lesson Two: Never slack on advocating for yourself. The majority of people you encounter in the private sector are not going to have your best interests at heart. Their inclination is to exploit you so that they can make a profit. Nobody's going to hand you anything, so you need to get in the habit of demanding it. And for goodness sake, never refuse a chance at advancement. They are rare and we have a long climb ahead of us."

Every day I learned something from Cassandra. She was a deeply compassionate soul, but not a pushover. While she could sympathize with tales of struggle and woe, she did not tolerate pity parties or victim posturing. Instead, she encouraged those around her to actively participate in changing the circumstances of their lives.

"We can't change where we came from," she liked to say, "but we *can* change where we're going."

I woke up every morning excited to go to work. I coordinated all aspects of Cassandra's schedule, handled event logistics, and supervised the interns. My duties weren't glamorous, but it was gratifying to know that every hour I spent at the office was creating a ripple towards the improvement of someone's life. I also took it upon myself to beef up OWN It's web presence, starting with a website re-design. The static site soon boasted a job board, video testimonials, an events calendar, and a message board. I even lined up guest editors to produce fresh content for a blog, each week representing a different theme.

I was logging over forty hours each week, but didn't mind at all. After such a long stretch of unemployment, it felt great to be busy. The work also helped distract me from the fact that I was thousands of miles away from the man I loved. The long-distance thing would have been a lot harder if I'd actually had time to miss Damion, but OWN It had become my new boo, requiring my undivided attention. Damion was making the most of the time apart as well, and had made solid progress on his book. The weeks were flying by, and with summer fast approaching, we'd be reunited soon enough.

Faby was thrilled to have me back in LA. Once I got settled in my new gig, she started lobbying for us to get a place together. Faby had been living with her parents in Pasadena for seven months and she was over it. Her commute to downtown LA was ridiculous, taking over an hour each way to go twenty miles during rush hour. I'd been commuting from my mom's place in Eagle Rock, and I, too, was over it. Life was too short to spend that much time in traffic.

"I've saved up a decent amount of money since I got home," Faby said. "I can spot you a few months rent if you need me to."

"Actually, I'm good," I said with a smile. "Ms. Ford is paying me pretty well to be her errand girl."

By June 1st we were moving into our new apartment in Westwood. The location was ideal—we could both get to work without having to get on the freeway, and the ocean was only twenty minutes away (ten minutes if I rode my bike). While the beaches in LA were nowhere near as clean as the beaches in Santa Cruz, it was great to be back on the coast. Great to be living with Faby again, too.

"I'm so glad we get to have one more year together before you join the ranks of boring, married folk," Faby teased.

"Ha, ha. Trust me, I would have been fine with a long engagement. We're hurrying down the aisle for practical reasons. As Damion's wife, I can be a consideration in the negotiation of any job offers he gets. And if he decides to stay in London, we'll need to be married in order for me to get a visa."

Faby frowned. "You know I'm Team Damion all the way, but you guys aren't really going to settle down in London, are you? Why can't he get a job here, like at UCLA or something?"

"He's looking," I said, "but jobs in academia are really competitive, especially in California. We'll have to see how it all plays out."

While I wholeheartedly supported Damion's pursuits, I did share Faby's concerns. Now that I was back "home," I was enjoying being around my friends and family. I had missed them. I also loved my job. What would we do if Damion's only prospects were in London? Could I really abandon what I was building here to join him, or ask him to do the same? What if we had to spend another year apart? Or more? Was our relationship strong enough to withstand an extended separation? Was I?

Chapter Thirty-Seven

Samantha

Another great thing about being back in LA was that I once again had access to a stellar music scene. I'd missed the cloak of a smoky club, the air around me vibrating with the pulse of bass or the melodic riff of a guitar. With so many great venues to choose from, there was always a band playing somewhere. I made it a point to get to two shows a week—so much better than watching television.

Celeste, one of our interns at OWN It, had been raving about this local band, Soul Fusion. They were playing at a bar in Santa Monica on Thursday night, so I decided to check them out. Faby was supposed to go with me, but she got stuck at work so I headed out alone. I actually didn't mind flying solo on my music missions—I liked having the freedom to leave when I got bored. Going out with Faby required a lot of stamina—she was always trying to close the damn club down. Not me. My days of partying until three in the morning were happily behind me.

I studied the flyers on the bar while I waited for the bartender to return with my beer; Soul Fusion's opening act would be taking the stage momentarily. Then I scanned the room for an open seat near the front. Since the bar was only at 30 percent capacity, I had plenty of options.

The house lights dimmed, signaling the start of the show. My drink almost slipped from my grasp when Tony appeared center stage, an acoustic guitar on a strap around his neck.

No. Fucking. Way.

I froze, afraid that any movement on my part would draw his gaze in my direction. Wow. I flashed back to the first time I saw Tony on stage, in a play at UCSC. He'd taken my breath away then, and had a similar effect on me now. Tony was right at home in the spotlight, and even though he'd lost some weight and was sporting a scruffy goatee, he was still one of the sexiest men I'd ever laid eyes on.

Jesus, of all the bars in this town, I just had to pick this one....

"What's up y'all?" Tony said, adjusting the mic stand. "How's everybody doing tonight? Are you ready to party?" His query was met with hearty applause. "Now that's what I like to hear. Indie artists thrive and survive on your support, so on behalf of my band, FourPlay, and our brothers from Soul Fusion, we'd like to thank you for coming out. Our goal is to make you glad you did."

Ha—Tony had a ways to go to meet that lofty goal. Seeing him filled me with a sense of foreboding and I was already regretting my decision to come to the show.

Tony scanned the crowd until his eyes landed on me. He paused, like he'd lost his train of thought.

Crap, I've been spotted.

"It's nice to see some familiar faces out there," Tony said, regaining his composure. "Make sure you stick around and say hi after the show." He winked at me.

Against my will, I nodded.

The band was a quartet made up of Tony (lead guitar), a bass player, drummer, and keyboardist. Each musician (with the exception of the drummer) took turns on lead vocals, and the guys were nailing their harmonies. They reminded me of a neo-soul version of the 90s Rock group Extreme.

Tony barely took his eyes off me the entire set, his penetrating stare igniting so many dormant feelings. Then he made a shocking and bold move that rendered me speechless.

"If my band mates don't mind, I'd like to deviate from the set list to play a song I wrote many moons ago about a girl who stole my heart in Santa Cruz, California. This one goes out to the one that got away."

> *Walking away that summer day, is the greatest regret of my life*
> *Misery is my punishment, for making the wrong woman my wife*
> *Every moment since, I've been hopelessly off track*
> *I'd give anything, anything, to have that one back*

I couldn't breathe. He had written a song about... me. And not just a song, but a beautiful, reflective, remorseful tribute to the love we'd shared. We might as well have been the only two people in the room as I met his gaze, allowing the memories to flood in.

The woman seated next to me tapped my arm. "Is he singing to you?" she asked.

190

I shook my head no. *I need to get out of here,* I thought. *Nothing good can come of this...*

I ended up ignoring my gut, though. I couldn't bring myself to leave in the middle of the show. The band was *good.* They closed out their set with a string of up-tempo reggae tunes that had the now-packed club on their feet, singing and dancing, myself included.

Before the applause had even died down, Tony hopped off the stage and headed right for me, leaving me no chance to escape.

"Hey," he said, staring down at me.

I was a collection of raw nerve endings. "Hey," I managed.

"Enjoy the show?" he asked.

"Yeah." *Small talk. Stick to small talk.* "Your band is great—you guys have CDs for sale?"

Tony smiled. "Yeah, backstage." He extended his hand. "Come on."

I stared at his outstretched hand. This was how it had all started the day we met. After taking his hand on the cliff that day, my whole life had changed. I didn't want to wander down that road again, but before my mind had a chance to intervene, my body responded. A few minutes later, I was seated on a couch backstage, being introduced to the band.

"Fellas, this is my good friend, Samantha," he said. "We went to school together in Santa Cruz."

I was almost offended by his introduction, the trite way he described what had gone on between us. But really, what was he supposed to say? There wasn't a soundbite in the world that could adequately describe what we'd been through together.

Shaun, the bass player, kissed the top of my hand. "Ah, 'the one that got away,' I presume? Very nice to meet you, Samantha. What a pleasure to have such loveliness in our midst."

Each one of them was a charmer, and they were having a great time battling to be the center of my attention. I was thankful for the group setting, as I wasn't quite ready to be alone with Tony. While I always knew there was a possibility I'd run into him now that I was back in LA, I was totally unprepared for it actually happening. But the only thing that seemed to be on the agenda tonight was some rock star partying. There were bottles of vodka and tequila at our disposal, courtesy of the club, and about six blunts on the table. Tony even offered me a line of coke.

"No thanks," I said, waving it away. I'd never had a desire to try cocaine.

"How about some E?" Shaun asked.

Hmmm. Now that was tempting. I'd had some fabulous experiences on Ecstasy. It was probably my favorite drug after marijuana, and would definitely take the edge off some of this awkwardness.

"Sure," I said, to everyone's surprise.

Shaun dipped into his stash and produced a tab of E for everyone. While we waited for it to kick in, we headed out to the bar to watch Soul Fusion's set.

Chapter Thirty-Eight

Tony

When I saw Samantha sitting in the crowd, I thought I was hallucinating. I had given up on ever seeing her again, having no idea what happened to her after she graduated from UCSC. But there she was, ten feet away, as beautiful as I remembered. When our eyes met, her surprise mirrored my own. Had she just randomly shown up at this bar, not knowing I had a show? What were the odds of that?

It shouldn't have surprised me though. Of course Fate would bring her back into my orbit. The strength of our connection was too powerful to ever truly be severed.

The months I spent with Samantha in Santa Cruz were the purest moments my soul had ever known. Years had passed and I still thought about her all the time. In the beginning, I prayed her memory would fade, that a day would come when I'd be able to get through a week without seeing a flash of her face, those lips, those caramel-colored eyes. But her memory persisted; she was a ghost that haunted me. In fact, the images deepened, increasing in clarity and pushing in at the most inconvenient times, like when I was making love to Angela. I have to confess, thinking of Samantha while in bed with Angela helped me perform my husbandly duties on more than one occasion.

In an attempt to rid myself of Samantha's ghost, I tried to teach my heart to hate her. But it didn't work. Her image was even stronger then—her kindness, trust, and forgiveness. My subconscious refused to let me betray her memory by making a lie of the love I felt, love that apparently I would always feel.

The irony was—I didn't feel anything nearly as strong for my wife. Angela and I had been unhappily married for three years now, a truly miserable existence. The two times I tried to leave her, she had attempted suicide. Fear kept me shackled to her side, as I was convinced that any attempt to liberate myself would be met with a similar response. So I shifted my strategy and focused on trying to get her to leave *me*. I committed myself to being the shittiest husband on the planet—withholding affection and sometimes sex, refusing to do any household chores, and blowing all my money on booze and drugs. That didn't work, so I kicked it up a notch and started the band, which kept me away from home most nights for gigs and rehearsals. For some reason Angela was able to tolerate having an absentee husband, and didn't give me much grief at all about my comings and goings. After a while I stopped trying to escape my loveless marriage. Our union wasn't ideal, and it certainly wasn't love, but we got along well enough and had built a life. Besides, if I couldn't be with Samantha, there was no reason to leave.

Then Angela got pregnant, and nine months ago she gave birth to our son, Justice. That kid was the new center of my universe, providing me with all the motivation I needed to stick it out with Angela. I grew up without my dad, and his absence left scars on my psyche. I wouldn't abandon my son. That was one promise I was determined to keep.

But seeing Samantha again... man. I felt like I'd been hit with a bucket of cold water. The proximity alone stirred up all those long-forgotten dreams, as well as sincere grief for what could have been. But I had to wonder—could it be again? Was Fate handing me a second chance at happily ever after, and if so, what was I going to do about it?

Samantha hadn't asked me about Angela, and I hadn't asked about her relationship situation. We'd just been hanging out with the band backstage, avoiding any touchy subjects. But now that the Ecstasy was starting to kick in, I was experiencing a surge of love and an irrepressible attraction. I no longer wanted to be in this smoky club, crammed in like sardines with sweaty strangers. I wanted to be on the beach with Samantha, listening to waves crash, engaged in one of our marathon conversations underneath the stars. There was so much I needed to say, and I couldn't wait another minute.

"Wanna get out of here?" I asked. "I'm craving fresh air and moonlight."

Samantha stared up at me with wide eyes—I could tell the E was kicking in for her, too. "You read my mind. Let's go."

Chapter Thirty-Nine

Samantha

Damn, I love Ecstasy. In my opinion, it was one of the best drugs on the planet. Unlike acid or mushrooms, I'd never heard of anyone having a "bad trip" on E. As the drug kicked in, all fear and uncertainty evaporated, leaving you with an overwhelming appreciation for all things. The primary effect was a powerful sense of happiness and well-being, a perception that all was right with the world. It was kind of amazing that a controlled substance could simulate… love. Scientists needed to figure out how to make Ecstasy safe and just add it to the water supply already, like they do with fluoride. The world would be a magical place if everyone felt the way I was feeling right now.

Tony and I meandered down to Santa Monica Beach, our path paved by moonlight. We stopped along the way for ice cream, which was an excellent idea. When you're on E, all five of your senses are heightened. My taste buds jumped for joy when they encountered my generous scoop of Rocky Road—the chocolate, marshmallow, and nut concoction was heaven on a cone. Each lick was practically orgasmic.

We held hands as we walked along the shoreline, magically transported to another time and place. Though almost midnight, the wind lacked a chill as it tossed my loose curls on the breeze. Eventually we sat down and started playing in the sand. While I marveled at the texture of the sand slipping through my fingers, Tony worked on a sculpture. Verbal communication up to this point had been minimal, but we were completely in sync and connected. Like no time had passed and no trauma had transpired.

"I'm so sorry," he said finally. He had sculpted a large heart out of wet sand and was carving our names into it.

"For what?" I asked. In my altered state, I was so beyond the need for an apology.

"I promised you a lifetime of love and I bailed," he whispered. "I let fear trap me into something wrong and walked away from the only thing that ever made sense. Not a day goes by that I don't regret the choices I made. I miss you all the time. I don't think I'll ever get over losing you."

I interlaced my fingers with his, my heart surging with love. "I don't think I'll ever get over losing you, either," I confessed.

Tony etched the words "destiny" and "purpose" into his sand heart. "I always try to find the lesson in things, but I can't figure this one out. I'm supposed to be with you, Sam. Every inch of me believes that. I've been lost and off course since I left Santa Cruz, numbing out my misery with drugs. I deserve better, Angela deserves better... We all deserve better."

"Life is too short to settle," I said, wondering if it was too late for us to make a course correction. Being with him again felt like... home.

Tony touched my face. God, I'd missed his touch. Nobody made me feel the way Tony did. Nobody.

"Everything's so complicated now," he said. "Even more than it was back then." He paused. "Angela and I have a child. A son."

The news should have devastated me, but thank god for the Ecstasy. Any potentially negative emotion was given a positive spin before I had a chance to experience it. As a result, the thought of Tony as a dad warmed my heart. "How old is he?"

"Nine months. His name is Justice."

"Justice... I love it. Do you have any pictures?"

Tony retrieved his wallet and handed me a photo of the most adorable little boy. Justice was a light-skinned version of Tony, with curly, blond hair. "Oh my god," I gasped. "He's precious."

"Thanks. He's my life. Justice showed me it was possible to love again after losing you."

I smiled. "He's a lucky little boy. I always knew you'd be a great dad."

I entered the time machine again and traveled back to another night, one that had ended in tears and heartbreak. Since Ecstasy also acted as a truth serum, I felt ready to unburden myself of the secret I'd been carrying for so long.

"We had a baby once," I said softly.

Tony looked confused. "What?"

"That day, outside of Damion's mom's house, when you told me there was no future for us... I was pregnant. That's why I forced Damion to drive me down to LA, so I could tell you."

"Are you serious?" The color drained from his face. "You're serious. God, Sam, why didn't you say something? That would have changed everything."

"How? What would you have done, huh? Moved both of your baby mamas in together to create a polygamous cult?" I giggled at the mental image. "Knowing I was pregnant wouldn't have made it any easier for you to leave Angela."

To my surprise, Tony didn't argue the point. "So, you had an abortion?" He looked crushed.

"No, no—I could never have aborted our baby, Tony. I had a miscarriage."

"Oh, babe…"

Tony pulled me into his arms. I'd buried the trauma of the miscarriage so deep; at the time I hadn't been strong enough to engage the pain and confront the loss. But safe in his embrace, buoyed by the effects of the Ecstasy, the emotions came pouring forth in a cathartic release.

"It was awful, Tony," I whispered through the tears. "It was the most horrible pain I've ever had to endure. Even though I was scared about having a baby so young and the thought of raising it alone, I wanted that baby so much. It was *ours*."

He was crying now, too. "I can't believe we had a child."

"It's my fault that we don't. I mean, I didn't even know I was pregnant for weeks. I was drinking, smoking, not taking care of myself. I was such a mess after you left…"

"Then put the blame where it belongs—on me. I should have been with you, taking care of you. I'm so sorry I wasn't there." He kissed the top of my head. "I am so sorry."

"And I'm sorry I didn't tell you," I said. "Regardless of what was going on, you had a right to know."

"I understand, and I forgive you."

"I forgive you, too," I said. "For everything."

And with that, any hatchets gathering dust in the corners of our hearts were officially buried. I'm telling you, Ecstasy is magic.

I let him hold me as we comforted each other, grieving together for the first time over the future we'd lost. As he rubbed my back, I was so grateful for this moment. The loss of our child was an event I hadn't yet fully healed from, probably because I hadn't been able to process the grief with Tony. I'd just taken an important step towards closure, and was slowly inching closer to whole.

"Let it go," he whispered. "All that guilt and pain you've been carrying… lay it down right here in the sand. It wasn't your fault. It was a cruel and terrible thing to have to go through, but it was *not* your fault."

The hurt and sadness began to dissolve at his command. Tony was right—I needed to lay it down. And for the first time, I felt like I finally could.

We remained locked in embrace for a while. Being in his arms was so… soothing. I had missed this so much—the ease of co-existence, the effortless way he was able to read my thoughts and give me exactly what I needed emotionally and spiritually. My soul felt light in his presence, fully anchored in the now, without regret about the past or anxiety about the future.

Tony noticed me shivering. "It's starting to get cold. We should get a hotel room. We can hang out, order room service, keep talking."

I pondered his suggestion. It would be several hours before I was in any condition to drive. "You know of a place that has 24-hour room service?" I asked. All of a sudden I *had* to have a cheeseburger and fries.

"As a matter of fact, I do. I'd kill for a cheeseburger and some garlic fries. You down?"

Wow, he could still read my mind. "You had me at cheeseburger," I said with a smile. The thought of crispy, golden fries became a beacon, and I happily followed him back toward town.

Chapter Forty

Tony

I did not expect to awake from our amazing reunion to find Samantha in the middle of a panic attack. She was mumbling to herself as she crawled around on the floor, a frantic search underway for articles of clothing that had been discarded the night before.

"Where is my damn bra?" she cursed.

I sat up and reached for her. "What is your rush? Come here—"

Samantha recoiled, like I'd struck her. "No, don't. I can't. I have to go." She abandoned the bra search and pulled her shirt over her head. "This was a huge mistake."

She may as well have been speaking in tongues—that was the most nonsensical thing I'd ever heard her utter. "What are you talking about? Last night was the one right thing I've done in a very long time. I've been dead inside, Sam. You woke me up. God, we've wasted so much time. Too much time." I blocked her path to the door. "I'm not letting you go again."

Samantha sat down on the bed and buried her face in her hands. "You don't understand. I can't."

"Look, I know you're scared. But this isn't going to be like last time. I'll leave Angela. Tonight. I'll petition for joint custody of Justice. Nothing is going to stand in our way. We belong together."

When Samantha lifted her head, tears moistened her cheeks. "Tony... I'm engaged." She met my eyes. "To Damion."

I laughed. She had to be messing with me. "Yeah, right. You're engaged? To Damion? How is that even possible? Isn't he in London?"

"He is. And so was I until about a month ago."

Damn, that Ecstasy must have been laced with something. I was *not* hearing this.

Samantha made a move for the door. I grabbed her again, a little rougher than I meant to, and forced her to face me. "I'm sorry, but you do not get to drop a bomb like that and run away before it explodes. What the hell? You couldn't have mentioned this last night?"

"I know. I'm sorry. I didn't know how to bring it up. Besides, you never asked about my relationship status. Not once."

It's true, I hadn't asked. I didn't want to know. I still didn't want to know. "Come on, it's not like you're engaged to some dude I never met before. You're with *Damion*. You should have said something."

"You are absolutely right," she said. "I've been exercising some extremely bad judgment since I saw you on that stage."

Bad judgment? Was she for real? If I hadn't been recovering from the shock of the news, I would have put my fist through the damn wall. I'd expected that she'd moved on, but I was not at all prepared for the words coming out of her mouth. Talk about emotional whiplash. All night I'd been on cloud nine, thinking our reunion was the start of a new chapter, a chance to make all the wrongs right. Was she really trying to tell me that she would rather be with Damion than me?

Chapter Forty-One

Samantha

Trying to get Tony to understand how I came to be engaged to his best friend was hands down the most uncomfortable and awkward exchange I'd ever had. As I tried to fill in the blanks of the past few years, he sat motionless on the edge of the bed, his expression barely masking the betrayal that deepened with each passing minute. I had hurt him. After all these years, I had finally succeeded in hurting him as much as he'd hurt me.

And he called me on it.

"You make it sound like I planned this!" I fired back, my voice raised. "I didn't know you were going to be at that stupid club. I didn't think I was ever going to see you again! And really, you have some nerve trying to paint yourself as the victim here. You wanna talk about hurt? I'm the one who's been hurt. If you hadn't abandoned me to begin with, I'd be wearing *your* ring on my finger."

"Yeah, yeah, I know—karma's a bitch. I'm getting exactly what I deserve. But of all the guys on the planet you could have moved on with, you pick Damion? That's like stabbing me in the back with a freakin' axe."

I tried to defend the indefensible. "It just happened. Damion and I got to be really good friends, and the friendship grew into… more. But we fought it, both of us did, for a long time."

"And now you're engaged."

I couldn't look at him. "Yes."

Tony sat back, arms folded across his chest. "I'm sorry, but after last night, there is no way you're going to convince me that Damion is anything more than a placeholder."

"We were on Ecstasy, Tony," I argued. "We can't trust what we were feeling last night."

"That's bullshit and you know it. What happened between us is as real as it gets."

Of course, he was right. Our connection was as strong as ever, which is how I came to find myself in this lovely predicament. "Look, I fucked up. I should have run when I saw you, not stuck around and dropped Ecstasy—"

"That's interesting. If you no longer have feelings for me, then why the need to run?" Tony challenged. "Why is being around me so dangerous?"

Those were fair questions. But answering them honestly would only make this situation worse.

"I made a terrible mistake, Tony. I'm with Damion now."

"So you keep saying. But do you love him?"

"Of course I love him!" I yelled, jumping to defend my relationship. And despite my recent actions, I meant it. "Damion has been in my corner and by my side through some of my darkest days. He is faithful, consistent, and loves me unconditionally. I have *never* known that kind of devotion."

Tony flinched. "Well, it's a pity you couldn't return it."

Ouch. It was a low blow, but that didn't make the statement any less true. "Take as many cheap shots as you want, Tony. You can't make me feel any worse than I already do. Trust me."

My words prompted a cease fire, and silence filled the air between us. Minutes passed as we stared at our respective spots on the wall. I couldn't do this anymore. I couldn't process what I'd done and argue with Tony at the same time. It was all just too much.

"So you love him," Tony stated. He appeared to be coming to terms with things. "Question is—do you still love me?"

Man, I didn't know *what* I was feeling anymore. "Of course I do. I mean, a part of me is always going to love you. But there's a difference between loving someone and making a life with someone. And Damion and I... we're building a life."

"I see."

More awkward silence. I was actually surprised by how calmly this conversation was proceeding. Tony wasn't throwing things; I wasn't crying my eyes out. I half-expected him to launch into some impassioned plea to win me back, but he looked... defeated. And for this, I was thankful, as I didn't have the energy to go many more rounds.

"Are you going to tell him?" Tony asked.

Tony's question drew my focus back to Damion. Jesus, what had I done? Damion would never forgive me for this. And why should he? I was not worthy of being his wife—I had proven that.

"I don't know," I whispered. I was stone sober now and starting to grasp the gravity of the situation.

"Well, whatever you decide," Tony said, "it's on you. Damion won't hear about this from me."

I don't know if that was supposed to make me feel better, but it did make everything real. "I have to go," I said, heading for the door. Tony didn't try to stop me this time.

Talk about a walk of shame. More like a sprint of shame. I fled the scene like the damn building was on fire and managed to make it back to my car before completely losing my shit. I caught a glimpse of my tear-streaked face in the rearview mirror and wanted to slap the woman staring back at me.

Great job, Samantha… You just torpedoed your best shot at happiness…

Chapter Forty-Two

Damion

After two years abroad, it was great to be back in the States again. Goldsmiths was on summer break, and I had six weeks in LA before I had to return to London and start the final year of my postdoc. I hadn't realized how much I missed home until I damn near broke down at the sight of my mother. I was ready for some TLC, home-cooked meals, and time with my girl.

I'd anticipated a passionate reunion, but Samantha had been acting strange since I got back, distant and distracted. I had planned to stay at her and Faby's apartment, but after the first night she suggested I crash at my mom's for a few days.

"Babe, I've got a major deadline at work that needs my attention," she explained. "As much as I'd love to play hooky and hang out with you, I need to fine tune the budget for a three million dollar grant. The proposal is due Friday."

"But I can help with that," I said, nuzzling her neck. "Grant-writing is one of my specialties."

"I appreciate the offer, but there's no reason for us both to be holed up in front of the computer. Go spend some time with your mom and catch up with your friends. As soon as this grant is done, I'm all yours."

"Hmm. If I didn't know better, I'd think you were trying to get rid of me," I teased.

"Never that," she assured me. "But I have a job now and I don't want Cassandra to see me slackin' cause my man's in town."

"You sure that's it?" I pressed.

"Yeah. I'm just stressed. I'll be in a much better mood after this proposal is submitted."

So I relocated to my mom's house in Culver City. Being home with my mom was actually kind of nice. I was a self-proclaimed mama's boy—it had been just the two of us for most of my life, and in many respects she was my best friend. Since I was sorting through some pretty complicated issues at the moment, I appreciated having access to the counsel of my most trusted confidant.

"The position at Oxford is still very much on the table," I explained over a large bowl of mom's signature gumbo, "but I feel like I should be focusing my job search on Southern California. Samantha loves her job, and we're going to be starting a family at some point. I want to raise our kids near their aunts, uncles, cousins, and grandparents—not five thousand miles away. Living abroad just doesn't seem like the move anymore."

"You realize I'm completely biased on the subject, right?" Mom asked. "I didn't want you moving to London to begin with."

"I know, Ma. And I love you for letting me go in spite of your personal feelings on the matter."

"I just want you to be happy, baby. Whatever makes you happy, makes me happy."

My mom was the most generous person I'd ever met, and unconditionally supportive of whatever goal I decided to pursue. I'm sure she raised an eyebrow when I called to tell her that Samantha and I were engaged; after all, she was fully aware of Tony and Samantha's history and the fact that she was the reason for my falling out with Tony. But whatever concerns she may have had, she kept them to herself and didn't pass judgment on the situation. Instead, she colluded with Samantha's mom and Faby to throw us an elaborate engagement party my first weekend back.

The party was huge, and all our friends and family were on hand to celebrate. There was more food laid out than I'd ever seen in my life, an interesting mix of southern BBQ and Filipino staples like *lumpia* and *pancit*. I met Samantha's mother and siblings for the first time; her family met my mom. At first it was overwhelming, all the hugs and catching up. But the party was a proper homecoming, just what my heart and soul needed after being gone for so long.

I was in the backyard manning the grill when I saw Ashley, Tony's sister, come through the back gate. I immediately handed the tongs over to my cousin and made a beeline for her.

"Ash," I said, picking her up for a huge bear hug. I planted a kiss on her dimpled cheek. "I can't believe you came."

"Of course I came," Ashley said. "You are family, D. Welcome home."

"Good to be home, Sis." I gave her another squeeze. "It is *so* good to see you."

Though I referred to Ashley as my sister, I thought of her more like a daughter. Tony's mom hadn't been much of a presence in the years before she passed, and Tony and I pretty much raised Ashley ourselves. I'd been looking after her since she was 12 years old, and would always have a special place in my heart for my baby girl.

However, her appearance amplified Tony's absence. Tony had been on my mind a lot the past few months, as I wondered how to bridge the distance between us given these latest developments. Now that word of our engagement was officially out, it was only a matter of time before the grapevine brought the news to his door.

"Did you tell Tony you were coming?" I asked Ashley. Maybe he already knew.

Ashley shook her head. "Nope. That's between you guys. I'm not getting in the middle of it."

"Always the diplomat," I said with a smile.

"I guess. I do think y'all are overdue for a conversation though. Seriously, Dame—you gotta reach out. You know he's too stubborn to do it."

"I know. You're right. I will give him a call before I leave town. Promise."

Samantha came outside and I motioned for her to join us.

"So that's the mythical Samantha…" Ashley said as Samantha crossed the lawn.

"Not what you expected?" I asked.

"Oh no, she's exactly what I expected," Ashley replied.

Samantha approached and I slipped my arm around her waist. "Babe, I'd like to introduce you to my baby sister, Ashley."

"I recognize you from pictures," Samantha said, extending her hand. "It's nice to finally meet you."

"Likewise," Ashley said, her smile warm and welcoming. "I was just telling Damion how happy I am for you guys."

"That means a lot, Ashley, thanks."

After a few minutes of small talk, Ashley excused herself. "I'm gonna go track down Mama Waters," she said. "I assume there's gumbo in there?"

"Two large pots," I said. Mom's gumbo was famous—all the neighborhood kids grew up on it. "And honey cornbread."

"Excellent. I'll be in the kitchen stuffing my face if you need me," Ashley said. "It was nice to meet you, Samantha."

Ashley disappeared inside the house. "Well, that wasn't awkward at all," Samantha said when Ashley was out of earshot.

"This whole scene is weird," I said. "I never imagined I'd meet your whole family for the first time like this…"

She gave me a kiss. "If it makes you feel any better, my mom and siblings approve."

"Oh yeah? They're not upset that I didn't formally introduce myself and ask for your hand before I popped the question?"

"If they are, they're doing a great job of hiding it. Everyone seems really happy for us."

I was relieved to hear that. Samantha came from a tight-knit family, and it was important to me that we had everyone's blessing. Now that familial support had been secured, the path to happily ever after was free and clear.

Okay, maybe not *totally* clear. There was still one important phone call that I needed to make.

Samantha had an odd reaction when I told her about my plan to contact Tony. "What's the matter?" I asked. "You don't think it's a good idea?"

"I mean, I understand your need to reconnect… I just think it's unrealistic to expect Tony to wish us well. He tried to knock you out the last time you saw him because he suspected you had feelings for me. Imagine what he'll do now that we're engaged."

"Probably try to knock me out," I said.

"So why even go there?"

"He's my best friend, Sam. There's almost two decades of history between us. Even if he slams the door in my face, I have to reach out."

Samantha was clearly uncomfortable, almost panicked, but she didn't try to talk me out of contacting him. I was thankful for her understanding—this conversation was long overdue. Tony and I probably wouldn't be able to repair our friendship under the circumstances, but I was going to give it one last try.

Chapter Forty-Three

Samantha

There was no escaping it—I was a woman on the verge of a nervous breakdown. I'd spent the past month trying to make sense of all that transpired with Tony that night. Was falling into bed with him a temporary lapse in judgment, or was there more to it? Obviously I still had a deep and active connection to Tony; what we shared was life-changing and part of my heart would always belong to him. No amount of prayer (and believe me, I'd been doing *lots* of praying) was going to change that.

But I loved Damion, too. The memory of Tony had kept me from entertaining a future with Damion for so long, but once I let go of the past and opened my heart to Damion, I fell hard. I wanted the life we were building, even though I'd just poured gasoline all over it and handed Tony a match.

Intellectually, it was a no-brainer which man I should be with. Over the years I had romanticized my relationship with Tony in such a way that it was larger than life. Like nothing would ever come close. But our union had never been tested in the real world, unlike the love I shared with Damion, which had been built with care on a solid and stable foundation. What I'd come to realize throughout the course of my remorse-filled analysis was that the reality of Damion was infinitely more powerful and promising than my mythical soul connect with Tony. I just wish I'd stumbled upon this epiphany sooner, before I'd committed unspeakable, unforgivable, relationship-ending acts.

I'd been going back and forth about whether to confess my indiscretion to Damion. At first, I was waiting for him to return to the States, since this wasn't the kind of conversation we could have over the phone or on email. But with each day that passed, I came up with more excuses to delay my confession. Didn't want to ruin his trip home, which he'd been looking forward to for months; couldn't drop the bomb before our engagement party, which our moms had been planning for weeks.

But despite all my rationalizations, the main reason I kept my mouth shut is because I was a coward. How could I look Damion in the eyes and tell him that the second he was out of sight, I'd cheated? There was no way he'd be able to forgive me, and that thought was truly terrifying now that I was certain I wanted to spend the rest of my life with him.

Living with a secret like this was miserable. The guilt was like acid eating up my insides as I simmered in a hell of my own making. It didn't help that there wasn't a soul I could talk to for advice or a third party perspective. Everyone loved Damion, and Faby would go ballistic if she knew what I'd done. (I actually feared her reaction more than Damion's—she *hated* Tony.) Besides, if I decided *not* to tell Damion the truth, I couldn't risk anyone else having knowledge of my betrayal.

Eventually it got to a point where I couldn't take it anymore. The secret was suffocating me. I had to tell someone and unburden my conscience, before I snapped and blurted it out, or lost my mind.

I reached out to DC, my best friend since childhood. Not only could DC be trusted to keep my secret, he'd probably refrain from judging me too harshly on account of his personal aversion to monogamy. He shook his head as I relayed the sordid details of my Ecstasy-fueled tryst.

"Well, damn, what did you think was gonna happen? Dropping Ecstasy with your ex? On some subconscious level, you had to know what you were getting yourself into."

"I know." I refilled my wine glass. I'd reverted to old patterns and was drinking a *lot*. "I'm a terrible person."

"You're not a terrible person, but you're obviously confused. Which one of these cats do you want to be with? If all the obstacles were to fall away and the slate were wiped clean—who would you choose?"

"Damion."

"Hmmm, that was quick. You sure?"

I had asked myself this question a hundred times. The last fifty, the answer had been Damion. "I'm sure."

"Then don't say shit, ever, to anybody," DC warned. "Even if Damion were able to forgive you, which he might cause the boy is *whipped* on your mulatto ass, he'll never forget."

"But I don't know if I can go on like this," I whined.

"That's something you're going to have to work out internally; it's your penance. In a way, confessing is the most selfish thing you could do. Your conscience will be clear, but in order to do so, you have to transfer that pain to another. If you're really sorry, and really want to be with this dude, and are *sure* this will never happen again, keep that shit to yourself."

I let out a slow breath. What he was saying made sense. "Okay."

"And stay the fuck away from that Tony guy!"

Chapter Forty-Four

Tony

When I got the call from Damion, asking to meet up, I was sure Samantha had told him what went down and that I was being lured towards an ass-whooping. But he didn't know; Sam hadn't told him. Damion's primary goal for this meeting was to mend fences.

We arranged to meet at our favorite bar in Santa Monica, right around the corner from the apartment complex we grew up in. I hadn't been to this neighborhood in years, and during the ride over I was flooded by fond memories of our youth. I rolled by the 7-Eleven where we used to load up on candy every Friday after we got our allowance. The park where we dominated afternoon pick-up games and were dubbed "Kings of the Blacktop." The half-pipe we used to hang out at during our brief skateboarding phase. I recalled the day I broke my ankle trying to ollie off a four-foot ledge. Damion had carried me four blocks from the skate park to the house.

I couldn't help but smile. *Well played, D.*

Damion was seated at a corner table nursing a Heineken when I arrived. He stood to greet me, but no dap, no hug, nothing. Times sure had changed.

"Thanks for meeting me," Damion said.

"Yeah, it's been a long time," I said, taking a seat.

"What're you drinking these days?" he asked, signaling the waitress.

"Henny and coke, usually," I replied.

"Been a minute since I had one of those. Remember that night in Vegas when we killed a fifth of Henny and I almost went home with a transvestite stripper?"

I laughed. "Ain't nothing to be ashamed of—he/she was fine. If I was single, I probably would have tried to holla at her, too."

"If you say so. I remember very little from that night—Hennessy goggles are no joke."

We ordered two Hennessey and Cokes for old time's sake. Something told me we were going to need several rounds to get through this.

"So how's London?" I asked.

"London's been good to me, man. 'Bout to wrap up this postdoc and hit the job market. How about you? What have you been up to the past four years?"

Man, had it really been four years? My life had become so monotonous and routine that each year blurred into the next. "Unhappily married to Angela, but resigned to my Fate. I'm pretty much a stay-at-home dad. I watch Justice during the day, and jam with my band at night."

"Wait, hold up. I have a nephew?" Damion asked, amazed.

"Yeah," I said, retrieving a picture of Justice from my wallet. "He's almost one."

Damion stared at Justice's photo with pride and love in his eyes. "Damn, Tone—you have a son! Man! Look at that smile! And that hair? What? Is he walking or talking yet? Tell me everything!"

I could talk about Justice all day, so the subject proved to be a great icebreaker as we reconnected and bridged some of the distance between us.

"I can't wait to meet the little man," Damion said.

Even though we didn't share DNA, Damion was the only brother I had, Justice's sole uncle. Despite all that had gone down, if anything were to happen to me, Damion was the only person I trusted to step in and be a father figure to my son.

"Yeah," I replied. "We'll set something up."

We were three rounds in before we got to the heavy stuff. But by then, I was so happy to be kickin' it with my bro again that most of my anger and hostility had evaporated. I'd forgotten what it was like to chill with someone who really knew me. I was able to speak candidly about my relationship with Angela, and not be judged. I could share my thoughts and fears, and have them met with compassion and understanding. My band mates were great to party with, but there wasn't any emotional depth there. They didn't have a frame of reference for where I'd been, and what I'd overcome along the way. With both my parents gone, Damion and my sister, Ashley, were all the family I had left. Now that I was a father, I had an even greater appreciation for what that meant.

"So about that elephant in the room," Damion began, steering us onto the subject we'd been successfully avoiding. "There's something I need to tell you about me and Samantha."

"About the engagement?" I asked, cutting to the chase. "I heard."

Damion was stunned. "You did? Oh."

"Yeah, good news travels fast."

"And you're cool with it?"

I was anything but cool with it, but Samantha had been very clear about what she wanted—which was apparently to marry Damion. I had already robbed her of one happy ending—I wasn't going to steal this one from her as well. I planned to take our secret to my grave.

"You know better than anyone that all I've ever wanted was for Samantha to be happy. I pushed her away so that she could find someone who would love her and take care of her. She found you." I forced the words out. "Just make sure you treat her right."

"I would lay down my life for that girl," Damion assured me.

"Well, hopefully it won't come to that," I said with a smile.

Though it killed me to envision a future without Samantha, I was strangely comforted by the fact that Damion was the man she'd chosen. He was a great guy—the best man I knew—and I had no doubt he would give her the life she deserved. Damion didn't have any baggage; he'd be able to provide for Sam and make her the center of his Universe. What did I have to offer? I didn't even have a job. What judge would give me custody of my son when I couldn't even demonstrate stable income? In the cold, sober light of day, I had to accept that leaving Angela meant limited access to my son (assuming Angela didn't try to cut me out of his life altogether). I loved Samantha, but Justice was my priority. I couldn't lose him. That boy was my world.

I made a choice all those years ago and set this chain of events in motion. As counterintuitive as it felt, I needed to let Samantha go.

Chapter Forty-Five

Samantha

The hours I spent waiting for Damion to return from his visit with Tony were torture. This was the moment of truth. For the past year, I had been deferring to the wisdom of the Universe to direct my path. Well, the Universe had deemed it necessary to bring Tony and I together again, and was also determined to bring Damion and Tony back together. All of this had to have happened for a reason, and it was time to see how it all played out. In a way, the decision had moved out of my hands and into Tony's. He had the power to end things for Damion and I... The question was, would he?

I braced myself when I heard Damion's key in the door. I'd asked Faby if we could have some privacy, so she was out with my friend Rob, who she'd reconnected with at the engagement party. The request was self-preservation on my part—if the shit went down, I could only handle being cussed out by one of them at a time.

Damion greeted me with a huge smile and kiss, which told me everything I needed to know. Tony had remained true to his word and kept our secret. I almost collapsed under the weight of the relief I felt, but thankfully I was already in Damion's arms. Which is apparently where the Universe believed I belonged.

"I take it things went well," I said, as we settled on the couch.

"Yeah, surprisingly well. He already knew about the engagement."

This wasn't news to me, but I feigned the appropriate amount of surprise. "Wow. And?"

"He told me to treat you right."

"That was big of him," I said. The back of my head was resting on Damion's chest and I was so glad he couldn't see my face.

"I thought so. He's still with Angela, and they have a son, Justice."

Again, I had to fake an appropriate amount of surprise. "I guess they were able to work through their issues. I hope they're happy."

"Happy may be a stretch, but Tony seems committed to being a father."

"That makes sense," I said softly.

Damion gave me a gentle squeeze. "You okay? Can't be easy to hear Tony has a kid… you know… considering."

Being able to work through my feelings about the miscarriage was the one good thing to come out of that fateful night with Tony. Those wounds had finally started to heal. "That's all in the past," I insisted. "I've made peace with my Tony stuff. And from the sound of it, you have, too."

"Yeah, I think we're good. Tony and I have a ways to go before we're back to the way we were—if it's even possible to reach that place—but I'm happy that the lines of communication are open. He wants me to come by and meet Justice before I head back to London."

That caught me off guard. I hadn't expected Tony to jump to rekindle the friendship given recent events. "Really?"

"I know, it surprised me, too. I expected him to be mad... to have *something* to say about our relationship. But he really seems cool with it."

"Well, if that's the case, I'm happy for you," I said. "I know how difficult this estrangement has been."

"This is kinda weird though, right?" Damion asked.

That was the understatement of the century. "Don't question it," I said, "just be happy."

That was certainly the approach I planned to take. I'd dodged a bullet and been granted a second chance at happiness. A chance to prove that I was worthy of Damion's love. In a weak, nostalgic moment I had almost thrown it all away, but I'd learned my lesson. The past belonged in the past and I would do better this time around.

The End

Samantha

I slowly made my way down the aisle, rose petals littering the sand beneath my feet. A small collection of our nearest and dearest formed a semi-circle around the altar, where my groom awaited. I was so nervous, unable to lift my eyes to meet the supportive smiles of our guests. After the long and winding road our love had taken, we had finally arrived at this moment. There was no turning back now.

I handed my bouquet to Faby and looked up into my future husband's eyes. Tony beamed back at me.

"Friends and family," the minister began, "thank you for joining us today to bear witness to the union of Samantha and Tony. These two stand before you—"

A ringing phone interrupted the minister's opening address. I glanced in annoyance at the assembled guests, but they were all smiling back at me, as if they couldn't hear the phone. "Is someone going to answer that?" I asked.

The phone continued to ring. I opened my eyes and noticed the flickering light on my bedside table. My phone was actually ringing.

"Hello," I said. I wanted to move into consciousness and away from the wedding dream as quickly as possible. I'd been having a version of the same dream for the past five days, not exactly a comforting image as I counted down the days to my actual wedding to someone else.

"Hey." The voice on the other end was soft, but familiar.

How did he get this number?

"Tony." I glanced at the neon green numbers on the alarm clock. "Do you know what time it is?"

"Yeah, I know. Sorry. I just wanted to talk to you... you know... before your big day."

I clicked on the light. I was alone in my hotel room in Santa Barbara, just nine hours away from becoming Mrs. Damion Waters. Six months ago, Damion and I set a wedding date, and with Faby's help, I had planned a simple beach ceremony to exchange vows and formalize our union. I had fully committed to this course of action, and had been free from second thoughts and lingering doubts... until this past week. But as the date approached, signs kept cropping up that brought my thoughts back to Tony. The dreams had been bad enough, but I was unprepared for the effect hearing his voice had on me. Why was the Universe testing me like this?

"What do you want, Tony?"

"Are you sure you want to go through with this?" he asked. His tone wasn't accusatory, hurt, or hostile. He sounded like a concerned friend.

"Yes," I said. "I am marrying Damion tomorrow." I voiced the words with a lot more confidence than I felt.

"All right then, that's that." I heard him take a sip of something. "I guess all that's left is for me to wish you both the best."

"Thanks," I said.

A long, painful silence ensued, as we sat on the phone listening to each other breathe. Then I heard the phone click and the call disconnected.

I lay awake for the rest of the night, listening to the waves lap against the shoreline below. The hold Tony had on me was aggravating. We'd gone our separate ways and passed the point of no return, but he was still messing with my head. There was no future for us—I was clear about that. But the memory of him, and what we'd done, was preventing me from having a future with Damion.

I'd tried to erase all evidence of the indiscretion from my mind, pretend it never happened. I'd convinced myself that by devoting my life to Damion and committing to our future, I could somehow make amends for my betrayal. But I was starting to feel like I'd never be free from the guilt. Ever since that night with Tony, I'd been running—running from my feelings, running from the truth, and damn near racing down the aisle. I was so tired. I had to stop running. I had to stop before I ruined everyone's life.

Just before sunrise, I put my wedding dress on. I stood on the balcony of my hotel room and watched the sun come up, the morning light casting a glow across the landscape before me. It was a beautiful day for a wedding. We were scheduled to meet on the beach at 11 a.m., and then have a reception brunch in the hotel restaurant. I imagined Damion in his room, a few floors below me. He was probably sitting on his balcony, too, anxious with anticipation. Had he received a 2 a.m. phone call from Tony as well?

I knew what I had to do. We couldn't build a life on a bed of lies.

My sister found me on the balcony in my zombie state, and I sent her down to the beach to get Damion. By the time he arrived, I had slipped out of my beautiful, silk dress; it now hung, lonely and unappreciated, in the closet. I couldn't wear it a second longer—I felt like such a fraud.

Damion knew something was up the moment he entered the room. I was sitting on the couch in my bathrobe, shoulders slumped in defeat. For some reason, he didn't seem surprised to find me in this condition.

"What's up?" he asked, taking a seat beside me.

Oh god, he's going to make me say it. He's really going to make me say it.

"I… I can't…" I managed to choke out.

"Can't what?" he probed. "Marry me today, or marry me ever?"

I looked into his patient eyes. He knew the answer. As we stared at each other, tears gathered on the rims of my eyelids. The hurt and disappointment on his face was killing me, but I just couldn't live this lie a moment longer.

He drew in a deep breath. "Ooookay," he said, the first syllable drawn out in mild disbelief.

The tears were flowing freely now. "I love you so much, Dame. Please believe me when I say that, because it's true. You have made me happier than I've ever been. But I can't shake this feeling that we're meant for something… else. As much as we love each other, we're still settling."

"Settling? Wow, thanks, Sam. I was going to give up everything for you. It's nice to know you were just 'settling'."

"That's what I mean though. You shouldn't have to give up anything to be with me. You should take that position at Oxford. Everything you've done the past two years has been working toward that goal. You can't pass on this opportunity, not for me. Especially when I'm having all these doubts and reservations."

"And how long have you been having these doubts and reservations, huh? 'Cause this is the first I've heard of them." Anger shattered his stoic façade. "I'm standing here in a damn tuxedo, Sam. Our family is down there waiting for us, expecting a wedding. Why are you just now saying something?"

"I know—I shouldn't have let it get this far. I thought I was experiencing a normal case of cold feet, and that it would pass. But I've been up all night trying to dispatch some serious anxiety and it's not going away." I paused. "Deep down, I know getting married would be a huge mistake."

"I see." To my surprise, there were no counterarguments or impassioned pleas for me to reconsider. Damion either agreed with me, or had finally tired of my indecisiveness.

"Please don't hate me," I begged.

He loosened his tie, as if it were strangling him. "I could never hate you, Sam. To tell you the truth, I've known something was off for months. But I ignored my gut because I wanted this so badly. But if you don't want it…"

231

"I wanted to want it," I said softly.

"Right," he said. "Not exactly the same thing."

His heart was broken, but as awful as it felt to be the cause of such suffering, I knew I was doing the right thing. I needed to set Damion free so he could have the life he deserved, with a woman who was actually worthy of his love.

"You okay?" I asked.

"No," he said. "But I will be."

After I got dressed, Damion pulled me into one last embrace. I held him tight, thankful for the love and friendship of this amazing man. Then, hand in hand, we made our way downstairs. We broke the news to our family and friends the same way we'd gotten through all of our highs and lows over the past four years... together.

Did you enjoy this book?

If so, please leave a review at amazon.com.

Thank you!!!!

Discussion Questions

1. Damion and Samantha fought their feelings for each other because of Samantha's previous relationship with Damion's best friend. Is your best friend's ex off limits? How should you handle it if you *do* fall for your best friend's ex?

2. Samantha brought a lot of baggage into her relationship with Damion. Did she get involved with Damion too soon after her relationship with Tony? How can you tell if you're really over someone and ready to move on?

3. Damion and Samantha were both in their early 20's when they got engaged. Were they too young to be contemplating marriage?

4. Samantha blamed her one-night-stand with Tony on the Ecstasy. Do you think she would have ended up in bed with him even if she was sober? Are there people from your past that you just can't stay away from, no matter how hard you try?

5. Damion was going to turn down an excellent job opportunity in order to be with Samantha. Was that a foolish move? What kinds of sacrifices are reasonable for couples to make or expect when trying to make a relationship work?

6. Tony believes that Samantha is his soulmate. Should Tony have fought harder to be with Samantha? Are there forces strong enough to keep soulmates apart, or is this perhaps a sign that they *weren't* soulmates?

7. Tony ultimately felt that remaining a presence in his son's life was more important than being with the woman he loved. Did he make the right choice? Should parents stay together for the sake of the children, even if they don't love each other anymore?

8. Did Samantha make the right choice by deciding to leave Damion? Should she have come clean about her affair with Tony?

9. If Samantha *had* come clean about the affair, do you think Damion could have forgiven her? Is it possible for couples to rebound from a cheating incident, or is that the ultimate red flag?

10. If you could write an alternate ending for this novel, what would it be?

Samantha's story continues in

SOUL MATES

Some people are lucky enough to find the love of their life... several times.

Email **author@stephaniecasher.com** to join the **Soul Mates** mailing list and be notified when Book 3 is available for purchase!

Also Available from TPC Books

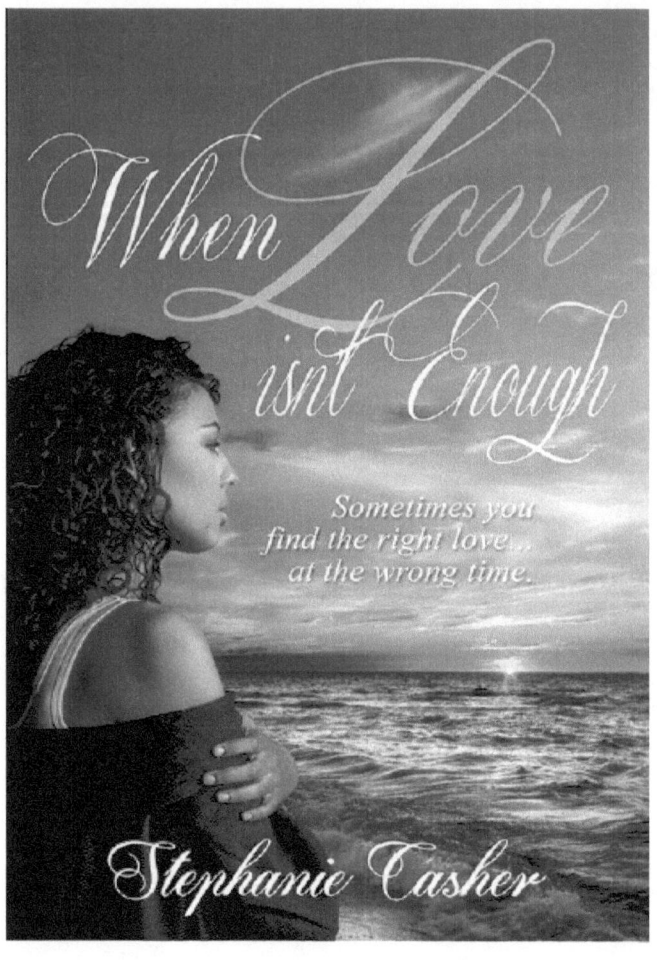

When Love Isn't Enough
by Stephanie Casher

A heartbreaking tale of true love, terrible timing,
impossible choices, and how you find the strength to
go on when you discover that sometimes,
love just isn't enough...

One Blood
by Qwantu Amaru

A supernatural curse terrorizes a group of
people unaware of their hidden connections.

SELLOUT
by James W. Lewis

SELLOUT follows these three individuals and the con-
sequences of dating outside their race. In the quest to
find what they think is missing in their lives, they encounter guilt, fear, and mess they never anticipated…
including murder.

A Hard Man Is Good to Find
by James W. Lewis

An erotic romance about a woman who meets
the man of her dreams with the exception of one
major issue - his refusal to have sex with her!

F.A.T.E: From Authors to Entrepreneurs
by Stephanie Casher, James W. Lewis & Omar Luqmaan-Harris

In November 2010, three authors stepped off the long, twisty
road toward traditional book publication, and charted a new
course under the umbrella of their own creation,
The Pantheon Collective (TPC).
Read how it all began...

For ordering information visit:
www.pantheoncollective.com

www.ingramcontent.com/pod-product-compliance
Lightning Source LLC
Chambersburg PA
CBHW050026180626
46810CB00002B/595